Secrets of the Underdark

J.D. Crist

Copyright © 2026 by Pumpkin Head Publishing

All rights reserved.

No portion of this book may be reproduced or used in AI in any form without written permission from the publisher or author, except as permitted by U.S. copyright law.

No portion of this book may be reproduced in any form without written permission from the publisher or author, except as permitted by U.S. copyright law.

Dedication

Thank you to my husband and amazing family, who continue to support my author journey. To all my readers, who continue to come back for more, none of this would be possible without you.

This book is based on the coal mines of West Virginia. I have nothing but respect for the brave men and women who work in those dangerous conditions every day. While this story may be fictional, I understand how dangerous the everyday work they do is. This book is also dedicated to all those brave workers and the resilient people of West Virginia. It is your strength of character and heart that inspired this location for the next installment of the rebellion.

Trigger Warnings

This story is a bit darker than Chains of the Union (Book 1). Please make sure you read the trigger warnings below and protect your mental health.

OR

Please enjoy this menu of things that I wrote about. You're welcome!

- Graphic violence with a pickaxe
- Attempted Rape (not involving MMC)
- Forced Breading
- Sexual Restraint
- Sexual Dominance

LEVEL 6
"The Pit"

- Speakeasy
- Red Light
- The Stalls
- Elevator
- Incinerator
- Bollgerts

Prologue

My adoptive father's voice droned on, but I had stopped listening. It was always the same with Blaylin. No one respected him, and I needed to fix it. He needed an heir, and I still hadn't proven myself. The people were plotting against him, and I needed to put them in line. The same things were repeated over and over for as long as I could remember. In truth, I wanted no part in any of it. I cared about nothing that was here, least of all him. The only person I had actually cared about died twelve years ago, and everything good in me died with her.

A banging on the door stopped Blaylin's ramblings as he yelled for them to come in. I didn't move, remaining still as a statue as I stared blankly ahead.

"President Blaylin," a soldier said in a rushed tone. "Governor Samuel from The

Union has arrived. He is waiting at the entrance."

A smile spread across Blaylin's face, and I knew he meant something evil. Yet, I remained emotionless. I should have felt something. Governor Samuel was my birth father after all, and I knew whatever Blaylin was planning would lead to his death. However, Samuel was also the man who had an affair with my mother, allowed her to be killed, and sold me to the president like a trinket he was glad to be rid of. Never once had he checked on me or tried to contact me since the day he dropped me off. A better person would have felt some emotion. Empathy, sorrow, hate, something - but I felt nothing.

"Bring him in," Blaylin said with glee. "Escort him to the meeting chambers."

The soldier nodded and rushed out of the room, shutting the door behind him. Blaylin stepped in front of me and gave me a cold, calculating look.

"It is time," he said in a firm tone. "Time to see if you are my son or his."

I remained motionless as he nodded in approval. He turned to leave, and I immediately followed behind him, my pickaxe firmly in my grip. When I was a teenager, Blaylin forced me to work in the mines for several years to build character. In truth, I think he was disappointed that my gift wasn't strength and he decided to force me to become the muscle he needed. After that, I kept it but for a different purpose. Its weight and swing were familiar to me, a part of me. Instead of using it to break the earth, I now use it to break bones and end lives. I had a feeling that I would be using it for that purpose later today.

I followed Blaylin through the tunnels and into the meeting chambers. Blaylin climbed onto the small stage and took a seat in his chair, which looked more like a throne than a chair. I stood at the base, the dutiful guard dog always on duty. We didn't have to wait long before the doors burst open and Governor Samuel strolled in with a small group of guards.

I barely paid attention as he tried to kiss Blaylin's ass with false compliments and promises. The man was scared, and I could sense it without even looking at him. As soon as he offered the soldiers to Blaylin's army, the arrows whizzed through the air and killed them all. It was no surprise. We had heard about the fall of The Union days ago. Blayin had received orders that anyone found fleeing was to be killed. Samuel would have been better off wandering the wasteland for the rest of his days. But his pride wouldn't have allowed him to stoop that low. He craved power and stability. A feat that would lead to his death in just a few moments.

And then it happened, the silent signal. Two soldiers stepped forward and forced Samuel to his knees. I took my time walking to him. I had pictured him when I was a child. I thought he would have been a large man, a force to be reckoned with. But the man before me was nothing but a pitiful shell of a human being.

"Son," Samuel said in a shaky voice as he stared up at me. Fear was pulsing in his eyes as he tried to pull at my heart. Little did he know that there were no emotions there to pull on. "I'm sorry about your mother and sending you away. I had no choice. If I hadn't, Lillian would have killed you."

The silence hung thick in the air as he waited for me to respond. I had no intentions of it as I tightened my grip on the pickaxe and prepared to swing. But then she flashed into my mind. A little blonde girl was sitting with me as she listened to my story about how I got here. I told her what I knew about Samuel and my mother. If anyone understood my pain, it was her. She had listened as I talked, placing her small hand on my arm to both encourage and comfort me.

"I'll never forgive him," I finished, wiping tears from my face with the back of my hand.

"You must," she said softly. "Not for them but for you. You deserve better than to carry all that hate and anger around."

The memory faded, and I found myself looking down at Samuel, kneeling on the floor. He didn't deserve my forgiveness. Yet, I couldn't stand the thought of her being disappointed in me, even if she was dead.

"Father," I said, causing him to look up at me with a flicker of hope. "I forgive you."

I watched as he let out a sigh and visibly relaxed. He thought that my forgiveness would save him. When he tried to stand, the soldiers pushed him back down to the ground. I raised my pickaxe just as he looked up at me and brought it down with all my force. It sank into his skull, and his body went limp. The soldiers held him still as I pulled it back out and walked back to my position, the blood still dripping to the floor and forming a small puddle where I stood.

"Excellent!" Blaylin clapped from where he sat. "You have finally proven your loyalty."

I felt no joy in his words and stayed where I was.

"Face me," he commanded. I did as he said, remaining silent. "I have another job for you," Blaylin said as I turned. "There is an illegal speakeasy being run in the pits. I have had soldiers trying to shut it down for months with no success. The incompetent fools have been able to do nothing. Tonight, you will monitor the pits, locate the speakeasy, and kill all those who are participating in its activities. We need this problem shut down before the start of the new term."

I nodded again and turned back to my original position. A couple of servants had begun clearing away the bodies, and I watched as they dragged Samuel's limp corpse across the stone floor. I would be taking more lives tonight, and that was something I could look forward to.

Chapter 1

Life in the mines wasn't easy, but it was all I had ever known. I sat in my tiny room, the walls feeling like they were closing in on me as I waited for time to pass. I had already worked a full day, but it was almost time for my second job. As if on cue, the lights cut out and the room became eerily silent. This was the way of it. At the exact time every night, the power was cut to The Pit. They said it was because the coal supply was running low and they couldn't keep the power running all night.

It was a plausible story, but everyone down here knew the truth. They cut off the power to control us. Only those of the upper levels had continuous power. Ours was cut off, and we had a strict curfew as a result. We were required to remain in our living quarters after lights out, no exceptions. Not that it stopped us. It may have been too dark to see anything, but that didn't mean we couldn't find our way around. I made my way over to the small, old, wooden chair and sat. I had to wait an hour before heading out, and there was nothing to do in the dark but sit and think.

    My mind drifted to the surface, as it did most of the time. What it must have been like before the Great War to live where there was always either sunlight or moonlight. Our ancestors believed in a simpler way of life, according to the history books. Small towns had once been spread through the mountains where people knew each other, and even if they didn't, they looked out for one another. The primary source of work back then was what it is now, mining coal. That is what had saved us. When the bombs started falling, the people fled to the mines and hid in the earth to survive.

    When the fighting stopped, the surface was destroyed, and they were forced to make homes underground. Over the years, they connected the mines and formed The Underwatch. On paper, it was a community where everyone was equal and worked together to survive. That may have been how the founders intended it, but the message had gotten lost over the years. Now, those on the upper levels lived in luxury provided by those beneath them. The lower you were, the worse your conditions, and I was at the lowest point, known fondly as The Pit.

But even compared to the other residents, my living situation was abysmal. With no family and refusing to take a husband, President Blaylin had made it his personal mission to make my life hell. When I was found as an infant, abandoned in the tunnels, I had been taken to his home to be raised; not that I saw much of him. Blaylin had servants take care of me as he was too important for such things. I was a burden to him from the moment I was discovered. Orphans with no family to claim them are unheard of in The Underwatch. Those with children received an extra stipend that no one could refuse. Yet, I remained unclaimed.

It didn't help that I refused to conform to what was expected of a good citizen. I cussed, fought, and refused to do as I was told. To say I was a rebellious child would be an understatement. I was kept locked inside the President's cavern and forced through lessons and punishments that were designed to break my spirit. My teachers would constantly tell me that if I didn't stop resisting their lessons, I would end up alone. What they didn't know was that, despite being locked away, I had managed to make a friend. A boy named Egon. When I snuck out after hours, I found him doing the same. We played and talked, each happy to have someone else in the prison we were trapped in.

    A tear ran down my face when I thought of Egon. Egon wasn't an orphan like me, but was purchased by the president to be his heir. The pressure to conform was greater on him than it was on me. Still, we took enjoyment in our young friendship, depending on each other to remain sane when we were pushed to our breaking point. However, even that was eventually taken away from me.

    When I was thirteen, President Blaylin had summoned me from my chambers early and told me that he was done supporting me. My refusal to conform, combined with my subpar gift, made me too much trouble, and he was done with me. He sent me to The Pit with nothing but the clothes I was wearing and said if I refused to live by his rules, then I was old enough to be on my own. I never got a chance to say goodbye to Egon. I searched for him for a few years, thinking he must have faced the same consequences as I did, but I never found him.

President Blayin had sent me a monthly allowance until I was sixteen and old enough to work. The allowance hadn't been enough to provide even the basics. I had learned from the start that I would have to find other ways to make enough to survive. I thought things would change when I was old enough to work, but they remained the same. President Blayin always made sure I was paid very little, expecting me to crack under the weight of it, but I refused.

I would never forget the day that Taylor came to me. He was old enough to be my father, with kind eyes and weathered skin. He worked as a miner by day but had also earned the president's wrath. His pay was always being docked for one reason or another, and he found himself unable to support his family with even the basics. His grandfather had been the first to run the speakeasy, a bar of sorts that ran after curfew, where folks could go to relax, blow off steam, and enjoy a stiff drink. It was located in an abandoned mine that the government seemed to have forgotten existed.

Taylor offered me a job as a waitress. He would give me a cut of the earnings in exchange for helping him run the place and taking care of the customers. It wasn't a lot, but it was enough to make sure I could survive. I accepted immediately, and he explained to me how to find my way through the dark. After that, every night, I left my room an hour after curfew and went to the speakeasy. I would work until closing and make it home just in time to sleep a few hours before my day shift started.

Every year, I feared I would finally get the assignment that felt like a death sentence: surface work. Honestly, I was surprised I hadn't been assigned already. President Blaylin hated me, but I suppose watching me suffer was more enjoyable for him. Still, every year when I was told my new assignment, I braced myself for the worst. The goal was always to return to the surface one day. They continuously sent a group of about twenty people to see if the land was habitable. To date, none had survived.

I let out a sigh as I stood from my chair and stretched. It was time to go to work. Slowly, I opened the metal door of my room just enough to slip out into the tunnels. My fingers immediately found the small carving on the stone that would lead me. I began to make my way through the tunnels swiftly, my fingers never leaving the wall as I followed the map that was carved into it. Everything was going just as it always had. Suddenly, I ran into something hard, stumbled back, and nearly fell. I steadied myself, terrified that my hand would leave the wall, and I would be lost in the dark.

"What the fuck?!" I yelled before I could stop myself.

"You're out after a curfew," a deep voice bellowed, which caused terror to spread throughout me.

Blaylin had been sending soldiers for months to find and shut down the speakeasy, but each had been easily bought off with a few jars of shine. But something about this man sounded different, deadly.

"So are you," I replied firmly.

"Perhaps I can help with what you are looking for."

A bright light turned on, and I lifted my free hand to shield my eyes.

"What the fuck is wrong with you?!" I screamed.

My body went rigid as a large hand grabbed my chin and turned my face. I hated when people touched me. Despite my trying to resist, my gift would push their emotions into my mind. Thankfully, I had mastered it enough to stop the memories from bombarding me. I braced myself for the bombardment of this stranger's emotions. Shock overtook me as I felt nothing. Suddenly, I became aware that he was still holding my face and staring at me. Embarrassment washed over me as I realized what he was looking at. A scar ran down my hairline on the right side of my face. I had gotten it sneaking around in the dark as a child. It had faded over the years, but was still clearly visible to anyone who looked directly at it.

"What's your name?" the man asked, his grip on my face loosening slightly. "None of your damn business," I spat back. "Now get your hands off me."

I pulled back, and he allowed me to free myself of his grip. I blinked and tilted to the side to try to get a glimpse of him, but the light immediately turned off.

"Go back to your quarters," he said firmly.

My blood began to boil. As if my smart mouth wasn't enough, I couldn't stand being ordered around.

"No."

"What did you say?"

I could hear the shock and frustration in his voice, but I remained firm.

"No," I repeated. "I have to get to work, or I'll starve. So, do you want your free shine or are you just being an asshole and making me late?"

His hand felt like a vice on my arm as he pulled me, and my fingers left the stone wall. My feet struggled to keep up as he dragged me through the tunnels. Despite his grabbing me again, I felt no emotions coming from him. I wanted to be grateful that, for some reason, his emotions stayed out of my head. Instead, terror filled me as he pulled me through the dark tunnels. I had no idea where he was taking me. Perhaps I was going to the cells. At least I would be given food there, so that was a bonus. I stumbled forward as he released me, and I saw the familiar faint red light that led towards the speakeasy.

"What the hell?" I asked, looking back into the darkness where I could sense the man was still standing. "You could have just told me you wanted the shine. No need for the theatrics."

"I don't want shine," the man grumbled, his voice dangerously low. "You said you have to work here to eat."

"Yeah," I replied, confused.

"Why?"

His question took me aback and gave me pause. I squinted into the darkness, and with the help of the dim red light, I could make out his figure. He was at least a foot taller than me, and judging by his width, could have easily broken me in two if he wanted.

"Your boss is a dick," I finally answered. "Baylin threw me out as a child and has made sure that I can't make enough credits to survive. So, I work here to make sure that I can eat."

He let out a grunt of understanding and disappeared into the darkness. I turned back towards the light and sprinted down the dimly lit passage, bursting through the door of the speakeasy. Taylor was already behind the bar and looked at me with concern. His skin was still covered in the black coal dust from a day of mining. I tried to steady my nerves as I made my way over to the bar and collapsed onto a stool.

"Drink," I said without looking at him.

Taylor immediately put a glass on the bar and filled it with what looked like water. As I lifted it to my lips, I could smell the burn that was getting ready to help ease my nerves. This was supposed to be sipped, but I needed it too badly to wait. I threw back my head and finished it in two big gulps. The burn in my chest brought me comfort as I set the glass back down on the bar.

"One more," I said. Taylor eyed me warily but filled the glass once more, and I immediately drank it.

"You want to tell me what's going on?" he asked as my breathing began to slow.

"I have no fucking idea," I admitted as I set the glass back down on the bar. "But a new soldier is roaming the tunnels, and he scared the shit out of me."

Chapter 2

"He scared you?" Taylor stuttered as he poured me another drink and one for himself.

Taylor knew me better than anyone else, and I did not often experience fear. I picked up my cup and swirled its contents just as he did. Setting my cup back on the bar, I stood up. For most people, that amount of shine would have made them feel tipsy. I had been drinking it for so long that it was just enough to take the edge off. I walked away from the bar and began setting up for customers.

I worked on autopilot as I set the chairs down on the stone floor and made my way over to the stereo. It was from before the Great War and looked like it belonged in a museum. I flicked on the power and watched as a green light lit up, confirming it was ready. I pressed the play button and felt myself relax as Highway to

Hell by AC/DC began to play through the crackling speakers. My eyes opened as the sounds of customers began to filter in.

The next few hours were a blur of serving shine, listening to people complain about work and the government, and making passes at me that I shot down with a smile. As midnight approached, people slowly began to file out and return home. Soon, there were just a few stragglers left, and I began to clean up for the night. The events with the guard in the tunnel left my mind as I swayed along to the music and wiped down the tables.

"If you wanted my attention, you got it."

I groaned internally as I looked over my shoulder to see Shawn standing there, eyeing me like a piece of meat. Shawn was attractive enough, but inside, he was hideous. I had overlooked it for a couple of months a few years ago. While I hated physical touch in general, sex was the exception. My gift was useful in this activity. Feeling the other person's emotions would help make my climax that much more intense. Shawn was the exception to the rule. He always enjoyed himself, leaving

me nothing but frustrated. I had hoped it would get better, but it never did. I ended things with him, but he didn't take it well. He had been trying to get me back ever since. Why he was so fixated on me was a mystery. There were tons of girls who wanted him for his looks, but he seemed determined to have the one who didn't.

"Just trying to finish up," I said as I lifted a chair and placed it upside down on the table. "Taylor has done last call. You should probably get heading out."

Shawn took a step closer, and the look in his eye told me what he was thinking. I didn't need to touch him to feel the lust and desire that was coursing through him. Normally, he was just annoying in his pursuit, but tonight was different. It was as if the shine had stripped away all his pretenses of being a gentleman, and now he was looking at me with a hunger that made my skin crawl.

"About done?" Taylor's voice rang out as he appeared beside Shawn. I let out a breath and nodded.

"Just a few more tables. I can lock up if you want to head out."

"I left your share on the bar," Taylor said with a nod. "We're closed tomorrow but will reopen after assignment day."

I nodded in understanding. Taylor rarely closed the speakeasy; his family depended on the income too much. But the night before assignment day, he always locked the doors. It was risky enough running this place; having people show up to assignment day hungover would have put more eyes on us than we needed.

"I'll walk you out," Taylor said as he looked over at Shawn.

I watched as Shawn's jaw tightened in frustration before he nodded and made his way towards the exit. I said a silent thank you to Taylor as he nodded and followed Shawn. Alone in the speakeasy, I turned up the stereo as someone named Ozzy poured out of the speakers. I danced around, finishing the last of the closing chores before switching it off. I found a small pile of credits on the bar. It was double my normal share, probably Taylor trying to make sure I wouldn't starve with the closing tomorrow night. I slipped them into the pocket of my jumpsuit and made my way towards the exit.

Something about the air in the tunnel felt heavier as I made my way out. The iron door shut behind me with a clang that sent a shiver down my spine. My fingers fumbled as I pulled the keys from my pocket and secured the lock. After testing the door to ensure it was secure, I found the indent on the stone and turned to begin my walk through the dark.

"We didn't get to finish our conversation."

My heart leaped into my throat as I took a step back. My first thought was that the guard was back. I watched as a figure stepped out of the dark and into the red glow. It was immediately obvious that it wasn't the guard, but I felt no comfort in the person who now stood before me. Shawn looked crazed as he continued to stalk his way closer. I thrust my hand into my pocket, planning to grab the key and lock myself inside the speakeasy. Shawn moved faster than I expected, and just as my fingers touched the cool metal of the key, my head slammed into the metal door.

"No running or hiding," Shawn growled as he bent down over me and grabbed a handful of my hair.

I held back a cry as the pain shot through my scalp, and he pulled me up and forced me to look at him. His breath clung to my skin as he breathed hard, his lips inches from my face. I struggled against him, trying my best to force him to let me go, but it only caused his grip to tighten. With his free hand, he grabbed my throat and held me firmly in place. Immediately, my mind was invaded by dark feelings of lust and desire. He was pressed against me, and I could feel his length against my lower stomach.

"Shawn," I choked out as I tried to pull his hand away from my throat. "You're hurting me."

"Good," he sneered. "Maybe if I hurt you, you will stop trying to pretend that you don't belong to me."

His choice of words did not escape me. I didn't belong with him; I belong to him. I began thrashing more violently, kicking and hitting with everything I had. Shawn pulled me away from the door for a moment, only to slam my head into the metal door. My vision immediately blurred, and he allowed me to fall to the ground in a crumpled mess. I felt around on the stone floor, trying to find anything to defend myself. Shawn appeared on top of me, his legs on either side as he held my hands above my head. The sound of a sharp slap filled the air, and moments later, I could feel the burn of it on my face. The taste of copper filled my mouth.

Before I could register what had happened, I heard the fabric of my tank top rip. The fabric around my left shoulder fell loose, and I continued to struggle against his grip. In all the ways I thought my life would end, being raped and beaten by a man like Shawn in the tunnels was nowhere on that list.

"So beautiful," Shawn growled as he leaned down and began nipping at my exposed flesh. I knew it wouldn't be long. His free hand was already roaming my body, feeling my breasts through the thin fabric of what remained of my tank top. I kept fighting, even though it was proving useless. If he was going to rape me, I wasn't going to make it easy for him. "Mine," Shawn said in a voice that sent a cold shiver down my spine. I let out a cry of pain as he bit into the skin on my shoulder. I could feel the warm blood running down my flesh as his bite broke the skin. When Shawn sat up, I could see the blood running down his mouth as he smiled at me like a wolf who had caught a rabbit. I knew he was an asshole, but I never realized how deranged he was.

"Now, how about you be a good girl and..."

Shawn's weight disappeared from on top of me as a large figure knocked him to the ground. I scrambled backward, my back finding the stone wall as I watched the fight happen. Shawn was on the ground, and the large guard was on top of him. His fists were pounding into Shawn's face with such force that I could see the blood splatter in the red light. The whole scene seemed surreal. Shawn's body was limp, but the guard kept punching. I tried to press myself further against the wall, my shoes scraping against the stone floor. The guard stopped his assault midswing and looked at me. The haunting glow of the red light made me feel as if a demon was staring me down.

I held my breath as he slowly stood up and walked over to where a pickaxe lay on the floor. Never taking his eyes off me, he walked back over to Shawn. I watched as the guard lifted the pickaxe above his head and brought it down onto Shawn's skull. I swear I heard the pickaxe hit stone as it went clean through. I remained frozen as I watched him place his foot on Shawn's throat and, with a couple of strong pulls, remove the pickaxe.

The air seemed to chill around me as the guard began walking slowly towards me. Shawn's blood and matter dripped from the pickaxe like a menacing warning of my own fate. My vision blurred again, and everything spun around me. I felt myself falling towards the floor as my vision went black. Fate has a funny way of things. I thought I was going to die after being raped. Not that taking a pickaxe to the skull was on my list either. At least, I wouldn't have to watch him kill me. Maybe it would be like drifting off to sleep and just never waking up.

Chapter 3

Was being dead supposed to hurt this much? My head felt like it was splitting in two as pain throbbed in my skull. I moved slowly, pressing my hands against my head and letting out a heavy sigh. I was alive but barely. I sat up, wincing as my body seemed to hurt everywhere. Peeking open my eyes, I found that the light was on. I had no idea what time it was, but it was clearly daytime.

The events of the night before suddenly came rushing back. The look in Shawn's eyes, the feeling of his hands on my body, the guard pounding his face, and then killing him with a pickaxe. I forced my eyes to open the rest of the way despite the pain and looked around. I let out a small, surprised gasp when I realized I was in my room. Normally, I hated being in here, but the shabby surroundings suddenly seemed beautiful and comforting.

I had no idea how I got there, but I was home.

My eyes swept over the small room, taking in every inch. My gaze froze, and my heart thudded against my chest when I reached the door. In the bright white light, he was even more intimidating. The guard stood there, his pickaxe leaning against the wall beside him. I glanced down, expecting to see the dried blood and gore from last night, but found it had been wiped clean. My eyes wandered back to the strange guard. He stood with his arms, which were probably the size of my torso, crossed over his broad chest. His dark eyes stared at me in a way that made me pull the blanket up closer to my body.

"Thank you," I stammered after a minute. He cocked his head at me, as if confused by my statement. "For saving me," I clarified.

"I cleaned your wounds," he said, his voice void of all emotion. "You will need to bandage your shoulder and take pain powder."

"I'll be fine," I insisted, still clinging to the blanket. "Those things cost too much." Anger flashed in his eyes as he took a step closer and uncrossed his arms. "Are you telling me that even with moonlighting at a speakeasy, you can't afford bandages or headache powder?"

I nodded, my voice refusing to work as his words came out with a touch of anger and danger. "I make just enough to feed myself and pay the required taxes," I said softly. Normally, I didn't feel so much shame about my situation. I was surviving, and that was an accomplishment. Something about this strange guard made me self-conscious, and I hated it.

I watched as he looked over at the small counter in the corner of my room. My food was neatly lined up on the shelves above the counter, the little of it that I had. He walked over, picked up the moldy, stale bread, looked at it with disgust, then set it back down. Other than that, I had half a package of stale crackers and two expired cans of meat. It wasn't much, but it was enough to keep me alive.

"The work day starts in an hour," he said flatly before walking back to the door and picking up his pickaxe. "You should get dressed."

Without another word, he opened the door and slammed it behind him. I winced as the sound echoed in my head, intensifying the pain. Carefully, I slid out of bed and placed my feet on the stone floor. The heat of the stone felt uncomfortable against my bare skin. Living underground meant no airflow, and the heat was trapped. On the upper levels, the ventilation systems kept things comfortable, and the stone felt cool. However, in the pit, our ventilation was just enough to keep us from suffocating or cooking to death.

I moved quickly to my shelf and grabbed a clean jumpsuit and tank top. My body ached as I slid out of the ones from last night. I made my way over to the sink and turned on the old handles. The pipes rumbled for a few moments, and then murky water came out. I waited until the water ran clear, then clogged the sink and dipped a rag into the water. The warm rag helped relax my muscles as I wiped away the memory of the night before, then slipped into my clothes. As always, I didn't wear the top portion of my jumpsuit correctly. The long sleeves made the insufferable heat worse. The law only required me to wear the ugly brown thing. I tied the sleeves around my waist tight to keep them in place just as my door opened.

    I looked to see the guard walking in, a brown cloth bag in his hand. He dropped it on the table with a thud and looked at me. The silence felt uncomfortable as we just stared at each other. Without a word, he left, and I stared at the bag he had brought. I quickly made my way over to it and slowly peeked inside. My heart raced as I looked through the contents and pulled them out one by one. A tin of pain powder, brand new and still sealed, a loaf of bread that was still warm, three fresh apples, a full first aid kit, and a container of cooked pork. The contents of the bag cost more than I made in a year after taxes.

    I pulled off a bite of bread and placed it into my mouth. I let out a moan as the flavor exploded on my tongue, and my stomach grumbled for more. I carried all the items to my counter and placed them on the shelf. I grabbed my cup, filled it with fresh water, and then added a scoop of the pain powder. I drank it quickly just as the tone vibrated through the tunnels, signaling it was time for work. I broke off another piece of bread and slipped an apple into

my pocket before rushing out the door.

    I fell into the crowd as I made my way towards the elevators, eating the bread slowly. By the time I arrived, my stomach felt fuller than I ever remembered it being. I stepped onto the elevator with a group of others, and the metal door crashed shut behind us. I was working on level two this year - an easy job that I actually enjoyed helping in the archives. The only person I worked with was a woman named Ginny. She was a bit odd, but was a kind soul. She took the time to teach me how to catalog and retrieve collected items, and even encouraged my curiosity. Most people saw my curiosity as a fault, but not Ginny. She would answer my questions about the surface or about the period before the

Great War, and recommend things for me to read in the archives. She was old enough to be my mother, and I found a strange comfort in being around her.

She always spoke of the day I would be in charge, how much better my life would be, and I had given up trying to tell her that I wouldn't be allowed to stay. Tomorrow was assignment day, and, as always, I would be given a new assignment because my work was unsatisfactory; it

was just the president's way of keeping me poor and waiting for me to break. Ginny insisted she'd give me top marks and that I wouldn't be going anywhere, but I knew that whatever she reported, I wouldn't be allowed to stay.

The doors to the elevator clanged open as we reached the second level, and we all filed out. Up here, the reason for the jumpsuits was apparent. Every level had its own color. Most people up here wore yellow, the color of level two. Browns, like myself, were scarce as most of us ended up working in the mines. You could also find some red, green, and purple from the other levels, but never a gold. Gold was reserved for level one. Up there, it was said they didn't have to wear the jumpsuits; just a scarf or something of the correct color to show their status. Most people couldn't confirm if this was true, but I could. As a child, I thought only servants wore jumps. It wasn't until I was exiled to the pit that I learned the truth.

I made my way through the tunnels, the pain powder taking effect as I walked. By the time I reached the archives, I felt like I could function again. Ginny greeted me with a warm smile as soon as she saw me. She froze, and her hands flew to her mouth as she let out a gasp. I didn't have a mirror, but I could imagine my face looking horrible.

"I'm fine," I insisted as I smiled back at her. "You should see the other guy."

I laughed a little, knowing that I couldn't tell her the truth. Shawn was dead, killed by a pickaxe to the skull wielded by a demon who saved my life and took care of me.

"You are not fine!" she insisted, ushering me to a chair and making me sit.

"I am going to put in a request tomorrow. I know the law requires at least two successful reviews before you can move up a level, but surely they can make an exception. You are going to end up dead if you stay down there."

Ginny was busy rushing about as she brought me a glass of water and a thick, worn book. I looked at the cover, my fingers brushing against the worn words.

"Alice in Wonderland," I read out loud.

"Classic fiction," Ginny explained. "We have several copies, and this one has been put on the destroy list. However, it's still readable, so the thought of destroying it broke my heart. I thought you would like it."

I looked down at the book and felt tears sting my eyes. I had always loved reading, but books were not something I could ever dream of affording.

"Now, you will sit here and read today," Ginny continued. "But when we get back after assignment day, it will be straight back to work."

I let out a small laugh and nodded. There was no point in telling her that I wouldn't be back after tomorrow. For now, I would let her hold on to her hope. I leaned back in the chair and opened the book's hardcover. I was immediately immersed in a world with tricky cats and talking caterpillars. I grabbed the apple from my pocket and slowly ate it as I read. I hadn't realized how much time had passed until the tone echoed through the halls.

"That's time," Ginny said gleefully. "You go straight home and get some rest. I want you to tell me what you think of Alice's adventures when we meet again."

"I will," I nodded, closing the book and standing up. The soreness in my muscles had returned, but I ignored it as I pulled Ginny into a hug. "Thank you," I said softly.

Ginny hugged me back, her tight squeeze telling me that she knew there was a chance she wouldn't see me again. Her emotions washed over me, and I could feel her sadness and love swell inside me. When we separated, I could see the shine of tears in her eyes that she was fighting to hold back. With a nod, I clutched my book to my chest and walked out of the archives. I wanted tomorrow to be different. I wanted to believe I could come back here. My heart ached as I gripped the book and climbed into the elevator.

The elevator moved quickly down to The Pit, and I followed the others off. Everyone was somber as we made our way through the tunnels. There would be no joy or celebration tonight. Everyone would stay huddled in their rooms until morning. Each was trying to look their best and hoping for a chance to improve their lives. I had no such dreams. Instead, I would live through Alice's adventures until the lights turned off and hopefully fall into a dreamless sleep.

I pushed open the door to my room and immediately thought I was in the wrong place. My pantry shelves were full of fresh food, medicines, and self-care supplies were on the table. None of that mattered to me, though, as my attention was drawn to the bed. I slowly walked over and picked up the small blanket that had been laid out. It felt just as soft as I
remembered as I pressed my cheek

against it. I wasn't one to cry, but the tears immediately sprang to my eyes. It was the baby blanket I was found in all those years ago. I was forced to leave it behind when the president banished me to The Pit, and I thought I would never see it again. I crawled into bed, clutching the blanket and the book. For the first time in years, I felt a peace I thought was lost to me. I ignored the question screaming through my mind, refusing to let it ruin the comfort I felt. Eventually, I would need to figure out who had given it to me, but for tonight, I just wanted to enjoy a rare moment of peace.

Tucking the blanket under my cheek, I lay on my side and opened my book. There would be time for worry and questions tomorrow. Tonight, I would enjoy the comfort of my blanket, live in Alice's world, and feast like a queen on the food that had been brought here.

Chapter 4

As the light in my small room came to life, I clutched the small blanket tighter in my grasp. It was assignment day, and I would be forced to leave the comfort I had enjoyed the night before. Alice in Wonderland still sat on the table, its worn cover practically mocking me. My adventure into a strange land, level one, would not be as fantastic as Alice's.

Forcing myself to sit up, I carefully folded the baby blanket and tucked it under my thin pillow. I wanted to stay here today and hide from the world, with it safely clutched in my arms. However, that was not an option. If I didn't show up, Blaylin would send soldiers to arrest me for treason. While I wouldn't mind time in the cells, I knew that I wouldn't be able to take the blanket with me. For now, I needed to get up and prepare for a day of torture. I could crawl back into bed once I got my assignment done.

I walked over to the small counter and grabbed a pear off the shelf. I tried not to think of the soldier who was sure to have been the one to bring me everything. There had to be a sinister motive behind his generosity. Soldiers weren't kind to those in The Pit unless they wanted something. After allowing the water to run for a few moments, I rinsed the pear and took a bite. The juice rushed into my mouth, and the flavor exploded. Setting the pear back down on the counter, I chewed as I washed my face. It was pointless, but I expected nothing less. A permanent layer of coal dust covered everyone in The Pit. I could wash it off, but it would always come back. By the time I reached the top level, coal dust would already be clinging to my skin once again.

When I was finished, I picked up my pear and continued to eat as I slipped into fresh clothes and brushed through my short brown hair. I never understood why women grew it long, especially in The Pit. It was too hot to have all that hair insulating the top of a person's head. I had shaved mine just a few weeks after being sent down here. I allowed it to grow out a bit over the years, just enough to keep from being mistaken for a boy, but short enough to keep it off my neck. The underside was still shaved close, helping to keep me cool. Still, there were women with hair so long that it would have dragged the ground behind them if they didn't keep it put up.

The tone sounded just as I tossed the core of my pear into the trash. Usually, I didn't accumulate much trash; I found ways to reuse things to save credits. It was strange to see it was filling up so quickly. I made a mental note to go to the incinerator sooner. After taking a few steps towards the door, I looked back down at the cores that were in the bin. I picked them back up and set them in the sink. After my evaluation was complete, I would see if I could remove any remaining seeds. It was too dark and cramped for me to try to grow them in my room, but perhaps I could sell them for a few extra credits.

Out in the tunnels, everyone walked shoulder to shoulder as we made our way towards the elevators. The people of The Pit were always the first to be evaluated and assigned. We liked to joke that it was because the other levels wanted to sleep in, but there was probably some truth to it. It was well known that Level One would have a party tonight to celebrate another successful year. They would need all the beauty sleep they could get to be ready.

"Excuse me."

The voice beside me sounded weak, but I would recognize it anywhere. I smiled as I looked over at Taylor and had to hold back a gasp when I saw him. One of his eyes was swollen shut, his lip was split, and there were small gashes on his face that cut through the bruises that covered it. I knew that soldier was trouble. He had been kind to me, but must have really worked Taylor over for running the speakeasy. Gently, I placed my hand on Taylor's shoulder, causing him to look at me with his good eye.

"You're alright." He smiled despite how much I could see it hurt him. "I was worried about you."

"I'm fine," I assured him. "I'll make that soldier pay for doing this to you."

"No," Taylor said, shaking his head, his face serious. "Shawn did this to me."

"Shawn?" I gasped.

"As soon as we left that night, he attacked me from behind," Taylor explained. "He dragged me into the tunnels and left me for dead. A soldier found me and helped me home. I begged him to go after you. I knew Shawn would be waiting for you to come out."

My heart thudded in my chest as Taylor's words sank in. The soldier hadn't just saved me, but the only father figure I had. He had only come back to the speakeasy that night because Taylor begged him to... to protect me. I was walking on autopilot as I helped Taylor into the elevator, the slam of the door pulling me from my thoughts.

"He saved you," I finally managed as the elevator began to travel up.

"Not only that, but the next day he delivered us fresh food and medicines," Taylor explained.

The soldier I had watched beat Shawn bloody and bury a pickaxe in his skull not only helped me, but then took it upon himself to deliver us fresh goods. This didn't make any sense. He had to want something, but I still couldn't figure out what. What could he gain from helping the owner of an illegal speakeasy and me?

"Your name," Taylor said as if reading my mind. "I demanded to know what he wanted in exchange for helping us, and he insisted that all he wanted was your name."
"Why?"

"He wouldn't say," Taylor admitted. "But be careful, you know how men like him are. It can't be as simple as it seems."

Of course it wasn't, things in The Pit never were. The elevator came to a sudden stop, and the door slammed open. I held onto Taylor's arm as we walked off, following the masses down the tunnels.

Up here, everything was at its best. The air was noticeably cooler, and I was glad that I had opted to wear the sleeves on my jumpsuit today. It was still hot, but being accustomed to higher temperatures, I felt myself get a slight chill. Soldiers stood spaced apart down the tunnel, looking down at us as we made our way. To everyone up here, we were worthless and untrustworthy. Funny, seeing as we saw them the same way. My eyes darted to each soldier. I wasn't sure whether or not I wanted to find the one from the other night, but I looked anyway.

When we reached the end of the tunnel, we were ushered into a large cavern like cattle. Around the perimeter, tables were arranged by last name. You had to wait in line, then you were taken back to a small booth where a high-ranking official would read your review and inform you of your assignment for the upcoming year. Taylor squeezed my hand as he walked towards his table, and I headed for mine.

The lines were outrageous, as always. Thankfully, the process was fairly quick. Each person was only in the booth for a few minutes before coming out, and the next person was called. I let my mind wander to Alice's story, wishing I could escape to another world, as I took another step forward.

"Perhaps this year's raise will be enough that you can afford more than moldy bread."

I nearly jumped out of my skin as I turned to see the soldier standing beside me. His face was firm, and his emotions unreadable. Not surprising, considering my gift couldn't even read them the other night.

"Doubtful," I said, regaining my composure. "I'm just here to get my new assignment and head back to my room."

"You expect a bad review?"

"No," I laughed. "I'm positive I got a glowing review, but it won't matter. It's the same every year. Just another way the president reminds me he is in control. Either that or this will be the year he finally decides to send me to the surface and be rid of me."

I watched as his jaw tightened and he clenched his fists. Something about his reaction unsettled me. He had saved me the other night, but I saw that as a debt I needed to repay as soon as possible. Owing debts was dangerous in The Underdark, and I never let one hang over my head. But the soldier's reaction seemed more fueled by emotion than anything else. There was no reason for him or me to feel any emotion for each other, and the whole thing put me on edge.

"Bridgett Coal!" the official called out.

I took a step forward, eager to put distance between the soldier and me. A firm hand gripped my arm and caused me to stop. I looked back at the soldier, his face tight with so much anger that he looked as if he might explode.

"Stop waiting to die," he said through clenched teeth.

"Excuse me?" I shot back. He had no right to comment on anything about me, let alone my life or death.

"I saw it that night," he continued as he closed the space between us. "You talked while you were passed out, about that not being one of the ways you thought you would die."

"Not much else to think about for someone like me," I snapped as I pulled my arm out of his grasp and stepped back. "Not all of us get to live. Some of us have to fight to survive, and death is the only thing we have to look forward to."

Turning, I stormed away and joined the official before the soldier could respond. Sitting in the metal chair, I could feel my heart hammering in my chest as the official sat down and opened my file. He seemed to be taking his time as he flipped through the pages, scribbling things down. I had no idea what was taking him so long, but I wish he'd get it over with. He did this every year, putting on a show before telling me the same thing.

"Well, it looks like the archives were a good fit for you," he said as he set down his pen. "Ginny had nothing negative to say and even filed for you to be moved to level two."

"What?" I asked, leaning forward, positive I must have misheard him. I knew

Ginny gave me a good review; my supervisors always did, but I was always told the opposite on assignment day.

"The move request is being denied at this time," he continued as he handed me a sheet of paper. "However, due to Ginny's report, you will be receiving increased compensation. If you continue to have such reviews, the request can be reconsidered in a few years. Any questions?"

"Is this a joke?" I asked, looking at the paper. It wasn't just an increase; they were doubling my salary. Even with the increased taxes, it was enough to provide me with basic comforts that I had never been able to afford.

"I assure you, Ms. Coal, I don't waste my time with jokes," he said, staring at me with dead eyes. "You are dismissed."

I nodded and stood, still clenching the paper as if it might disappear at any moment. Back out in the main cavern, the voices around me sounded like a dull drone. I looked down at the numbers, trying to ensure that I wasn't seeing things.

"Bridgett!"

Taylor's voice cut through the fog of my mind, and I returned to the present.

"Yeah?" I asked, glancing up at him.

"Is everything alright?" he asked, concerned. "I'm pretty sure Ms. Henderson heard me calling you, and she can't hear anything." Fear washed over his face as he looked down at the paper. "Oh, no," he gasped. "They didn't assign you to the surface."

Shaking my head, I handed him the paper. If I were seeing things, he would tell me what it really said.

"This is amazing!" he said, his smile making him wince slightly. "Guess I'll have to find me a new waitress."

"Don't you dare!" I snapped. Taylor looked taken aback, the smile disappearing from his face. "It's a trick," I continued. "It has to be. Once I get comfortable, it will be ripped away just like always."

Taylor said nothing as he handed me the paper back. As we turned to leave, I spotted the soldier on the opposite side of the cavern. His eyes were locked on me like a predator watching its prey. I knew in my gut that he had something to do with this. I didn't know what game he was playing, but I intended to win. I would clear the debt and end whatever this was.

Chapter 5

The old bastard kept his word. I watched as she left the cavern, confusion and anger etched across her face. I had hoped she would be happy, but she was too smart for that. She knew something was going on, and, based on the way she glared at me, she knew I had something to do with it. When she finally broke eye contact, I turned to leave. No one else here interested me.

I walked down the tunnels, soldiers snapping to attention as I passed. A show of respect, but I could see the fear in their eyes. The only person who didn't see me for the monster I had become was her. I shook the thoughts out of my head as I pushed open the door leading to the president's cavern. It was my home or my prison, depending on how you looked at it.

A large home had been carved into the stone, complete with more rooms than he would ever need and balconies. The bright lights on the ceiling simulated sunlight, causing the grass and flowers to grow. There was no coal shortage; he was diverting the fuel to power his personal oasis. Normally, Blaylin would have been leading groups of aristocrats through the grounds, bragging about his accomplishments. However, the way the servants scurried past, some with fresh bruises, told me he was still inside and pissed.

Blaylin wasn't used to not getting his way, and I had destroyed everything early this morning. A smile played on my lips as I thought back to it. He had planned for me to find her and demand that she be allowed home. However, he underestimated the monster he created.

"You're late," Blaylin's sick smile greeted me as soon as I returned home. "Find anything interesting last night?"

"You know damn well who I found," I growled back. "You told me she was dead!"

"No," Blaylin corrected while waving his finger. "I said she was gone. You assumed that I meant dead."

"You sent her to The Pit to suffer!" I bellowed, my voice echoing off the cavern walls. "You have been torturing her for years!"

Blaylin wasn't affected by my temper. He looked almost bored as he rolled his eyes and stepped closer to me.

"I've been preparing her," he said matter-of-factly. "She is too strong-willed to fulfill her purpose."

"You did this to break her?" I nearly laughed, and Blaylin's face dropped. "She is more stubborn now than ever before. You made her stronger, not weaker. Whatever your purpose for her was, I'm positive she'll tell you to shove it up your ass!"

"Enough!"

I felt Blaylin's gift pressing down on me, forcing me to my knees. I tried to fight against it, but it was useless. He could make you feel as if you were trapped under a collapsed pile of stone if he wanted.

"She will submit," he continued. "And you both will give me a child that can take over once I'm gone."

"A child?" I said through gritted teeth as the pressure pushing down on me intensified. "You expect us to..."

"Demand!" Blaylin interrupted. My hands fell to the floor, holding me up against the pressure that continued to press down on me. This sick fuck had been planning this since we were kids. Bridgett wasn't like me; she still had light left inside her. I wouldn't let him take that.

"No," I said firmly.

"No," Blaylin laughed. "You think you can refuse me?"

"I am refusing you," I continued as my arms began to shake. "Do what you want with me, but you will let her live and be free of us."

"And why would I do that?" I could feel his hot breath on me as he knelt closer.

"She has already accepted her death," I continued, beads of sweat dripping onto the grass. "She would rather die than submit, and I will honor that."

"You'll what?" For a man who was so sure of himself, I could hear the quiver of fear in his voice.

"I will kill her myself," I grunted as the pressure intensified. "She will be free, one way or another."

For a moment, I thought my threat had been the final straw. The pressure forced me completely to the ground, and I locked my jaw to contain the scream of pain that filled my lungs. I wouldn't give him the satisfaction of hearing it. The pressure disappeared instantly, and I slowly took several deep breaths. Even if he killed me, his plan was over. He needed me to be the one to bring her back, to keep her in line.

"This isn't over!" Blaylin spat as he stormed away.

I sat on the grass, wiping the sweat from my face with the back of my hand. The heavy drops continued as my body tried to regain control after what had happened. "Yes," I finally breathed to myself. "It is."

After that, I had sent Blaylin a list of demands on how Bridgett was to be treated. That's when the cussing fit and the sounds of breaking glass filled the house. The poor servants bore the brunt of his rage, but after a few hours, I received a message from him saying he had given his word that it would all be done. Still, I had gone to the assignment chamber to make sure he followed through. I knew her assignment was only valid for a year, but I would do whatever was necessary to ensure that Blaylin did not go back on our agreement.

Chapter 6

Things were quiet after I returned to my room. After a few hours of pacing like a caged animal, I had a plan. Working in the archives did have an advantage I had never considered. All of the resident records were kept there. They were generally sealed off so that Ginny and I couldn't access them, but for the next few weeks, they would be open. All of the records would be updated, and we would be tasked with fetching and delivering them to level one. The soldier had to have a file, and if I could find it, I could figure out what he was up to and how to repay the debt. The only problem was that I still didn't know his name.

There was no way I was going to discover anything sitting in this room. I folded the assignment letter and slipped it into my pocket before grabbing my credits and the seeds I had plucked from the pear core. My mind was focused on my tasks as

I worked my way through the tunnels to the stalls. The line at the desk was thankfully short, and I breathed a sigh of relief. Standing still was not going to help me right now.

Once I reached the counter, Mary smiled at me. Mary was one of the unlucky. The radiation after the Great War had a lasting effect on everything. Some people, like me, gained a gift of some kind. Your gift determined your worth in society. The rarer the gift you possessed, the more prestigious you were. I had never met anyone with a gift like mine, but the rules didn't apply to me. Others, like Mary, received no gift and instead had some physical deformity. Mary, a sweet older woman in her sixties, had a large mass on her back that forced her to remain bent over. She never let it break her spirits, though, always speaking with a smile.

"New assignment?" she asked as she took my paper.

"Not this year," I smiled back.

Mary let out an excited gasp as she read over the paper. Her grin lifted my spirits as she input the information into her terminal and handed me a small bag. "Congratulations," she grinned. I took the bag, surprised by the weight of the credits inside.

"Payday is the same," she continued. "You can pick up your credits on the first of the month. Your taxes have automatically been deducted. However, any fines or penalties will be deducted from the next month's credits, no exceptions or extensions."

"Understood," I nodded as I slipped the bag into my pocket.

With a friendly nod, I turned and made my way into the stalls. Small stalls full of different goods were scattered throughout the cavern. Their merchants were calling out, announcing their goods, and trying to convince people to spend their credits. Shopping here was different than on level two. Up there, the stores were carved into the stone, and the merchants did not need to beg for business. But, just like with everything else in The Pit, the merchants down here had to do everything they could to survive.

I walked past most of the stalls, ignoring the cries of the merchants as I made my way to the back. Nothing about these stalls looked different, but I knew they were. The merchants back here weren't as desperate, preferring not to draw more attention than necessary. They dealt in forbidden items and stolen merchandise. They were also adept at looking the other way when someone's credits didn't match their income level.

"If it isn't my favorite barmaid." I rolled my eyes at Felix as he grinned at me with his arms spread wide. "What can I interest you in today?"

Felix was a smooth talker, but everyone knew to be careful with any deals they made with him. He followed them to the letter, so you had to be precise in your bargaining. The goods on display were mostly for show; Felix preferred to deal in rare finds and secrets. He claimed to have been born on Level 1, banished to The Pit after he got caught having an affair with a married woman. It was hard to tell if it was the truth or a story he made up to bolster his standing. Either way, it didn't matter to me.

I glanced at the table, pretending to inspect the goods he had on display. "You wouldn't know anyone who would be interested in purchasing seeds, would you?"

"Seeds, you say," Felix grinned. "Let's have a look?" I pulled the small bit of seeds out of my pocket and held them up. Felix leaned closer, taking a look at them. He made no move to touch them. It was understood here that goods changed hands only when the deal was complete. "Now, where did you manage to steal these?"

"Not stolen," I replied.

"Interesting." The way he looked up at me made my skin crawl. "I might be able to take them off your hands. How much are you seeking?"

"No credits," I answered as I closed my hand around the seeds. "Information."

"Well, this is new," Felix grinned. I watched as he picked up a dress and motioned to the back of the stall. "I do have a changing room in the back if you would like to try it on."

"Thank you," I nodded as I walked behind the stall and through a tattered curtain.

Like most merchants, Felix's home was directly behind his stall. This allowed him to stay close to his work while maintaining privacy in exchanges like this one. Felix followed me and motioned to a worn chair. I took a seat as he threw the dress onto a table and sat across from me.

"Now, what kind of information could someone like you be after?" he asked, crossing his legs dramatically.

"A name," I said firmly. "I need a soldier's name and anything you may know about him."

"A soldier," Felix nodded. "Can you be a bit more specific?"

"I don't know much," I admitted. "I think he's high ranking. I've never seen one carry a pickaxe before."

"A pickaxe?" Felix's face went white, and his cocky demeanor disappeared. I nodded and watched as he began to fidget in his chair. "You are part of a small group down here. Very few have seen the Captain and live to tell about it."

"The Captain," I repeated.

Felix picked up a glass with a shaky hand and took a sip of water as he nodded. "I only saw him once. There was a man who had recently relocated here for engaging in questionable activities on the upper levels. The way he did business made me look like a straight-laced citizen. I tried to warn him that he was causing too much trouble, drawing too much attention, but he wouldn't listen."

Felix paused and seemed to be reliving some memory in his mind.

"What happened?" Felix blinked and focused back on me.

"He kept getting bolder and bolder," Felix continued. "Soldiers were staying in The Stalls, their numbers growing every day. Then, the Captain arrived. He didn't say a word as he passed by me like a gollum with a pickaxe. The fellow tried to bolster himself up to intimidate the Captain, but the Captain didn't slow down. I watched as he swung that pickaxe and sank it into the man's skull."

Bile rose in the back of my throat. I had seen that before. The man I was looking for was the Captain, but I still didn't have his name.

"His name?" I insisted, holding up the seeds.

"Don't know," Felix sighed. "Some say the devil didn't give him one before he spat him into our world. But I do know that he is the only Captain."

It wasn't perfect, but it was something. I nodded and handed the seeds to Felix, then stood up.

"Be careful," Felix warned as I turned to leave. "I know you don't fear death, but messing with the Captain is a sure way to guarantee it finds you."

I nodded, trying my best to hide my annoyance. Why did everyone think I was so eager to die? It wasn't as if I sought out death. I just accepted that it was inevitable and what would finally free me from this miserable existence. Felix spoke of the Captain as if he were a demon from hell.

Like so many other people, he didn't realize that we lived in hell. Therefore, I had nothing to fear. I would find a way to repay my debt before the demon came to collect.

Chapter 7

Ginny wrapped me in a warm hug the second I walked into the archives. For the first time, I could see that even she was concerned I wouldn't be allowed to return. I hugged her back, and for a few blissful moments we stood in silence. When Ginny broke the embrace, I could see the tears welling in her eyes.

"We have a busy day ahead of us," she said, wiping her eyes. "All of the records will need updating from the assignment day."

I nodded as my eyes went to the stacks. Ginny was still talking, but my mind had already moved on. Reading personal files was forbidden, and I had never considered breaking that rule. However, it may be my only chance to learn more about the Captain.

"Bridgett, are you listening to me?"

My eyes snapped back to Ginny, who was looking at me with concern. "Where did that mind of yours go?"

After taking a deep breath, I began to explain everything to her—the night in the tunnels, the food, and the Captain. Ginny listened without interrupting, taking in every word.

"You know how debts work down here," I spoke. "I need to find a way to repay it before he decides to collect."

"And how do you plan on doing that? You don't even know his name?"

"If he really is the only Captain, then his personal file should be easy enough to find," I said meekly.

Ginny's face went white at my implication. She started shaking her head, her eyes no longer meeting mine. "It's forbidden," she said firmly. "And even if it weren't, you wouldn't be able to read the files. They are all written in some code."

"Code?" I asked, looking at the stacks.

"Follow me," Ginny instructed as she began making her way through the aisles. The personal files were stored deep in the archives, rarely requested, and even then only by high-ranking officials. I watched as she pulled a thick file folder off the shelf, its citizen number written on the front. Ginny quickly undid the string, pulled out a sheet of paper, and handed it to me.

A smile spread slowly across my face as I looked down at the dots and dashes. I recognized it from my time with the president. It was a required part of my curriculum. Morse code was a form of communication used long before the Great War. Now, it was used to keep normal citizens from learning government secrets.

The file that Ginny held was for a citizen named Mary Hemlock. She was thirty-two with four children. Her husband, Peter Hemlock, died in a mining collapse three years ago. Mary worked as a seamstress on level three and received death benefits from her husband's accident.

"I can read it," I said with a grin. "That bastard actually taught me something useful."

"Just because you can doesn't mean you should," Ginny insisted as she took the paper back and returned the file just as she had found it. "If you get caught..."

"It's the only chance I've got," I insisted as I stepped forward and took her hand. "Please, Ginny. I promise, once I learn who he is, I will stop and never look again."

Ginny seemed torn as she looked between me and the shelves. Finally, her shoulders relaxed, and I could feel that I had won her over.

"You will be in charge of the carts," she said firmly. "Same drill as last year. Load them one by one and deliver them to the magistrate. When the light flashes twice, take the next cart and return the previous one. Make sure the files are returned correctly, and you work *quickly.*"

I nodded in understanding as I grabbed the first cart and moved to the first set of shelves. Ginny twisted her hands for a few more moments and then disappeared. She understood why I needed to do this, but couldn't bring herself to be part of it. I moved quickly, checking the pages in each folder for a Captain.

I had just finished loading the cart with no success when the red light on the ceiling flashed twice. I moved quickly as I pushed the cart through the tunnels and arrived at the magistrates' cavern. The large glass doors seemed out of place as I pushed them open with my backside and pulled the cart through. The young woman sitting at the desk barely glanced at me before pointing to a spot on the wall. Thankfully, I had done this last year as well and understood what she meant. I pushed the cart to where she pointed and left without saying a word.

I raced back to the archives and repeated the process for the rest of the day. My legs were burning from rushing around and pushing the cart all day, but I ignored them. It wasn't very smart to think I would find anything on him today. It took two weeks for the files to be updated. Still, I held out hope as I opened the last file for the day. That hope quickly evaporated as I looked at the file for the sixty-five-year-old man.

When I returned after taking the cart, Ginny was waiting for me.

"I'll wait for them to finish and lock up," I offered as I walked past her and slumped down in a chair. "No need for us both to stay here."

"Follow me," Ginny instructed as she walked into the stacks.

Her voice held no emotion when she spoke, and her face had given nothing away. My curiosity piqued as I followed her through the shelves and back to where the personal files are kept.

"You told me your story," she said as she stepped forward and grabbed a file. "But in truth, I didn't believe it all to be factual. I knew you believed it was, but that's the danger of a child's brain dealing with trauma and abandonment."

I stood silent as she walked over to a shelf and grabbed a file. My hands began to shake as she handed it to me. I opened it and carefully pulled out the first piece of paper. My breath caught in my throat as I read my own name. I looked back at Ginny, but her face was still unreadable. My attention went back to the file as I read through the history of my life.

"Only, your brain didn't make up things to protect you," Ginny said after a moment. "You truly lived through all of it."

"I thought you couldn't read the code?" The question seemed out of place as it slipped out of my mouth. Ginny smiled, her face softening as she looked back at me.

"I said you couldn't read the code," Ginny corrected. "When you could, I knew I had to know the truth. You're not the only one who was raised by someone at the top and then booted for being different. Yours preferred to torment you, while mine pretended I didn't exist. All because I preferred the written word to any of those pompous ass hats they wanted me to marry."

"Ginny," I giggled as I slid the papers back into my file. I had never heard her speak in such a way, and it sounded funny to my ears.

"I never looked at it before today," she said as she took the file back and returned it to the shelf. "But with everything, I felt like I needed to help you."

"Help me?" I asked as I followed her down another aisle. Ginny moved quickly to a shelf and grabbed another file.

"This is the only Captain," she said, handing me the file. "I glanced through it and couldn't find anything useful."

My heart sank as I looked down at the file. I could feel any hope I had slipping away.

"That man is a monster," Ginny continued. "His kill record is in there, starting at the age of fourteen. All with that pickaxe he got after working a year in the mines at the president's orders."

I had seen him use that pickaxe. The image of it coming down on Shawn's skull flashed into my mind. I shook it away and turned my attention back to Ginny.

"But, maybe you will see something I couldn't," Ginny sighed just as the red light began to flash overhead. "I will go get that. I left a sack at the front desk for you, with more books that were ordered for destruction that I thought you would enjoy. Just return the bag and anything you don't wish to keep in the morning."

With that, Ginny walked past me and disappeared. I clenched the folder tightly in my grip before turning and heading towards the desk. Sure enough, there was a burlap bag on the desk; its contents were books. Without glancing at the titles, I shoved the folder inside and hurried out.

Most of the rush was over by the time I left, making it easy to navigate my way to the elevator. It felt as if everyone was staring at me, like they knew what I was smuggling. I walked quickly and felt the tension leave me as soon as my door was shut.

I made my way to the table and dumped the bag out. Three books spilled out along with the file. I stacked up the books and pushed them to the side, not even glancing at the titles. I had already untied the file and was pulling out the papers as I sank into the chair.

"This is it," I said to myself as I took a deep breath and focused on the paper. My eyes moved over the first set of dots and lines, my brain not believing what I was reading. "This isn't possible," I said as I reread the name a hundred times. I forced myself to continue, reading every paper in the file: his work history, kill list, known family, everything. When I finished, I felt as if I was going to be sick. I shoved the papers back into the file and put it back into the sack.

This had to be a trick. It couldn't be real. I had searched for Egon for years. That boy who cried when he saw the welts from my lashing when we were children. Who talked about escaping Blaylin and living free? He hated the blood and violence that ran this place just as much as I did. But, if this record was true, he was now the man who kept the blood flowing.

"No," I said, shaking my head. "It can't be."

But somewhere deep in my heart, I knew it was true. The way he had been so gruff with me the night in the tunnel, softening only after he saw my scar. He had helped me clean and bandage that cut. When Blayin saw me the next day, Egon had taken the beating, saying it was his fault. This was just another one of Blaylin's sick games. Egon had grown to be just like that monster, and now I was nothing but a toy for both of them to bat around as they pleased. I didn't like being played. It downright pissed me off.

"Fine," I said, clenching my fists. "Game on."

If they wanted to play, it was time they learned I was no longer that little girl. I had learned my lessons, taken my lumps, and was still standing. They were going to learn that I wasn't such a fun toy after all. After shoving the file back into the burlap bag, I turned my attention back to the books. My body shook with a rage that I knew wouldn't allow me to read, but I still picked them up one at a time, inspecting the covers. They were worn, yet still beautiful in my eyes. There was Dracula, Frankenstein, and How to Kill a Mockingbird. I added them to a small shelf where Alice rested, knowing that I would be reading them as soon as my mind allowed.

The room felt suffocating as I collapsed on the bed and pulled my blanket out from under the pillow. My anger had started to fade, replaced by a pit in my stomach and the burn of tears that didn't fall. Egon, my childhood best friend, had become the very thing we had both hated. I closed my eyes and let my childhood memories play freely. Not the beatings or constant reminders of how inadequate I was. I replayed the moments in the dark, where Egon and I pretended the evil we faced during the day didn't exist—a place where we were just two kids who dreamed and laughed.

Chapter 8

The week seemed to drag by. I returned the file to the archives and continued running the file carts. Ginny hadn't asked me about the file, though it seemed like she could sense my sour mood. I couldn't help it. It wasn't every day that the one person you thought was always on your side had died, but then it turns out he became a heartless killer. The rage I felt was like a coiled spring inside me. The memories of my childhood grew fewer and fewer each day, unable to quell the storm raging inside me. I felt sorry for the first person who triggered it and for all the anger unleashed on them.

Ginny seemed to sense what I was going through, so she kept her distance and our interactions short. I shoved the cart through the door of the archives much harder than necessary before spotting a group of soldiers standing with Ginny. I should have known that this would happen.

If Egon wanted to collect his debt, he could have had the guts to do it in person.

"Bridgett," Ginny said in a shaky voice. "President Blaylin has requested your presence."

"No thanks," I said curtly as I attempted to push the cart past them all.

I had no idea what this was about, but I didn't want any part of it. I wasn't in the mood to play another sick game for Blaylin and Egon to laugh about. One of the guards reached out and grabbed it, stopping me in my tracks. I gave him an icy stare and tried to push forward again, only for him to hold me in place.

"I'm afraid we must insist," he said in a tone meant to make me cower.

He obviously hadn't been told who he was dealing with. Instead, I rolled my eyes and released the cart, throwing my hands into the air. "So much for it seeming like a question," I huffed."

"Bridgett!" Ginny scolded, looking at the soldiers with concern.

Most citizens feared repercussions if they didn't treat the guards with respect. I, however, did not give a fuck. What else could they do to me? I shrugged as the soldiers began to usher me towards the door, surrounding me like I was a prisoner. I guess I was in a way. No matter what, Blaylin had control over my life. There was no escaping his torment, especially with Egon now joining in.

People stared at us as we made our way down the tunnels and to the elevator. I ignored all of them as the door closed and the elevator rose to the top level. Fewer people lingered in the tunnels once we arrived. Back down on level three, I knew that the rumors were already spreading about me being arrested. At least the people would get a good story out of my torment.

The guards led me down familiar passages and to the President's cavern. It hadn't changed at all since I had last been here. The lush artificial grass still grew, despite the claims of power shortages that forced people of the pit into darkness. The fountains still flowed with cool, clear water, despite the water in my room turning brown.

The contrasts made me sick as the soldiers led me into the manor. Again, nothing inside had changed. Artifacts and art adorned every surface, revealing the wealth and power Blaylin possessed. Such pieces should be for everyone to see, but he gladly kept them to himself and to those honored with a visit. The ghosts of my childhood still ran through the halls, laughter in the dark and screams in light. I pushed the visions away as the door to the president's chambers opened.

There he was, the great President Blaylin. He hadn't changed much since the last time I saw him. He had more grey around the temples, and his pants size had gone up more than a few numbers, but there was no mistaking that it was him. He grinned at me like a cat who had finally cornered a mouse as the soldiers escorted me in front of him.

"My dear girl." Blaylin's deep voice echoed through the chamber like nails on a chalkboard. My body begged to shrink away from him, but I forced myself to remain still. "It has been too long," he continued. "I hope you are doing well."

"What do you want?" My voice came out clipped. Each word dripped with the hatred I had been holding in for years. Blaylin's face dropped, and I could see the anger burning in his eyes. His mask had been stripped away, and the monster I remembered now glared down at me.

"Show some respect, you little bitch!" Blaylin snapped. "If you think your life has been difficult up to now, you have no idea how much worse it can get!"

A small laugh burst out of me as I stared at him. He had tried to break me for years, and now, he expected a smile and some words to have done the trick? Now that he saw it hadn't, he was going to try to scare me into submitting. He had another thing coming; I would rather die.

"I believe we've had this conversation before," I replied. "Right before you banished me to The Pit and made sure I wouldn't have enough to survive."

Blaylin's face grew red as his chest rose and fell with heavy breaths. He was losing it. I grinned, realizing that I had the upper hand.

"But I did," I continued. "Not because of you but despite you. Now, you summon me here for what? To see if I will play the game your way?"

"To warn you," he snapped.

"Warn me?" I laughed. "Warn me of what?"

"You have no idea the position you have found yourself in," Blaylin sneered. He felt like he was taking control back. Part of me was curious about where he was going with this, so I allowed him to continue. "Do you remember Egon?" Blaylin asked. My heart squeezed in my chest, and I could feel my heartbeat in my ears.

"That boy who lived here as well?"

If he thought I was dumb, I could play the part, for now. Perhaps I could learn something from his arrogance that could help me with what was to come. I had learned all his tricks with words when I lived here. Now I had the chance to use that knowledge for my own gain.

"Yes," Blaylin nodded, his confidence returning. "I'm afraid he's gone mad in recent years. There are rumors that he plans to kill everyone who knew him before, including you and me. I wanted to warn you so you could take precautions. I would even be willing to allow you to take up residence here once more. For your safety, of course."

There it was, the truth hidden deep under a lie and false concern. If Egon were really a threat to Blaylin, he would have had him eliminated immediately. He wouldn't be offering to protect me and allow me to return. Especially to the same place where, according to his file, Egon still resided. This was a trap.

"No, thank you," I bit back. "I don't believe being housemates with the man who seeks to kill me is the best idea. However, I would like to offer you shelter, Mr. President. My room is small, but it is the last place he would search for you."

My tone was sweet, but Blaylin could hear the condescension behind the words. His face flushed once more, but his mouth remained shut. For a man known for having plans for every scenario, this one seemed to catch him off guard. I couldn't help the glimmer of joy I felt at seeing his discomfort.

"What is the meaning of this!" I didn't have to turn to recognize the voice behind me. My fists clenched at my side as he appeared beside me, glancing between Blaylin and me.

"Just checking in on Ms. Coal," Blaylin grinned. "I wanted to be sure that everything was set right after that unfortunate clerical error."

I could feel Egon's eyes on me, but my gaze remained locked on Blaylin. The treacherous bastard was up to something. Either he was trying to confuse me, or Egon wasn't part of his scheme, as I'd originally thought. Either way, I didn't trust either of them and needed to get out of here.

"I have no idea what game you two are playing, but I want no part of it," I glared at Blaylin.

"Game?" Blaylin grinned. "I assure you, this is no game."

"I don't give a fuck what it is!" All of my rage burst out of me all at once. "I am not part of it. I want you both to leave me the hell alone!"

Blaylin continued to grin, but I could see the evil glistening in his eyes. "I'm afraid," he snarled. "That's not an option."

My fists balled at my sides, and my mouth opened to yell at him once more. Before the words could escape, a hand roughly gripped my hair, pulling my head back. In the next moment, I felt the sharp tip of a pickaxe pressed to my neck. I couldn't see the coward, but I knew it was Egon.

"We had a deal," Egan growled behind me. It took me a moment to realize he was speaking to Blaylin, not me. I strained to see Blaylin, but Egon's grip on my short hair was firm.

"I'm calling your bluff," Blaylin gloated as he leaned forward. "You could never..."

Before he could finish his sentence,

the pickaxe pressed harder against my delicate skin. I bit my tongue and squeezed my lips together, refusing to give either of them the satisfaction of hearing that I was in pain. The warm liquid running down my skin told me that I had been cut, but I kept my expression firm.

"STOP!" Blaylin roared, shooting to his feet.

The pressure of the pickaxe relaxed, but Egon continued to hold me firm in his grip. I didn't try to pull away, knowing that if I succeeded, I would impale myself on the pickaxe that was still dangerously close.

"Do you still think I'm bluffing?" Egon snarled behind me. "Do you wish to continue?"

"What do you want?" Blaylin asked.

On the outside, he still appeared in control, but his voice had a slight tremor, hinting at the fear he felt. I had no idea what Egon was feeling. Despite his closeness, I couldn't make skin contact to use my gift. Something about not knowing made the fear in my chest swell.

"A decree," Egon said, his stance firm. "Bridgett Coal is to be banished from ever stepping foot higher than level 2, even for evaluation day, for life. If this is violated, by choice or force, her life will be forfeit."

What the hell was going on? Egon had done so much to help me, and now he was banishing me. Not only that, but if I were forced to come here, I would still pay with my life. Even more confusing, Blaylin seemed to care if I lived or died.

"Fine," Blaylin said through clenched teeth, motioning someone to come towards him. A small figure appeared from the corner of the room, handing a piece of parchment to him. Blaylin barely glanced at it before signing it. "It's done."

"Give it to her," Egon growled.

The same man took the paper from Blaylin and held it out to me, his hand shaking. I took it, still unable to step away from Egon.

"Let me see," Egon commanded. I held the paper up for him to inspect, surprised at just how still my hand was. "Have Ginny file this personally," Egon instructed after a moment. I nodded slightly, showing I understood. I expected him to release me, but instead, I felt him lean closer, his breath warm on my ear. "You're free," he whispered just loud enough for me to hear.

A shiver ran down my spine at his words. Whatever the game was, it felt like he was telling me I had won. In the next moment, he released me, and when I looked back, he was several steps away. I glanced back at Blaylin, the anger radiating off him in waves. I still didn't understand what just happened, but I knew I wanted out. Without a word, I ran from the chamber, through the tunnels, and didn't stop until I was in the elevator. As the iron door slammed shut and I felt it begin to descend, Egon's words echoed in my mind.

"You're free."

Chapter 9

Walking back into the Archives, I felt my body begin to fail me. All of the stress and confusion had turned into exhaustion. Ginny was waiting for me as soon as I walked in and wrapped me in a warm hug. I leaned into her, having no strength of my own left: no fight, no anger, no fear, just nothing. After several moments, Ginny helped me to a chair, and I sat.

"What happened?" she asked as she began cleaning the blood from my neck.

"I don't know," I answered honestly, wincing as she dabbed at the small puncture mark on my neck. The pain reminded me of the piece of paper in my hand. "I'm supposed to have you file this."

Ginny took the paper, and I watched as her eyes rushed over the words. "Banished?" she gasped. "And killed if you go back, even unwillingly?"

"I'm free," I said barely above a whisper.

Ginny looked at me with a raised eyebrow. I could tell she was waiting for an explanation, but I didn't have one to give. I looked away from her, staring at the smooth stone floor. I heard Ginny walk away and return a few minutes later with my file. She set to work behind the desk, the keys on the terminal clicking away.

"It's finished," she said as she added the paper to my file and tied it shut.

My eyes were focused on her as she placed the file on the counter and grabbed my shoulder. "Are you alright?"

"How did you do that?" I asked. "Only the magistrate can update records."

Ginny looked back at the terminal, then at me. Her eyes were heavy with regret. "The orders were for me to file it. Breaking that would have put your life in danger," she said.

"That's not what I asked," I said firmly as I pulled away from her. "We run those files every year for days to get them updated because we don't have access. Yet, you just entered that like it was nothing."

Ginny looked hurt as I stood and took steps away from her, but I didn't stop. This woman that I thought I knew, that I trusted, had a pretty big secret that she had kept from me. She wasn't a woman banished to the archives by some rich family. She still had connections, privileges, and access. I had enough surprises for one day, and I felt like whatever this one was might be the one to break me.

"I told you that someone at the top raised me," she said slowly, almost as if talking to a scared animal.

I nodded but still took another step back. That didn't explain how she still had access to the system.

"Typically, the records are updated by the head of archives," she continued. "However, my father continues to punish me, hoping one day I will accept his terms."

"His terms," I asked, my voice shaking despite my efforts to keep it steady. "He is the magistrate who oversees records and law," she explained. "He arranged a marriage to a man who saw me as nothing more than a thing to be bred. I refused, but I had already been assigned here. So, to punish me, he forces me to deliver the records to him, claiming I'm too incompetent to handle the task. Every year, he adds new ways to make my life more uncomfortable in an attempt to make me accept the marriage."

"What else has he done?"

I watched as she walked slowly towards the door behind the counter and opened it. She had told me it was an old storage room when I started, and I had never questioned it. As the door opened, I saw the truth. A small bedroll was set up on the floor, clothing was piled, and a few other personal items were scattered about. It was obvious that she was living here. The room made mine look like a palace. Looking back at Ginny, I could see the shame on her face as she looked at her home. She closed the door and walked back to where she was before.

"My credits are deposited with him to pay back a debt," she explained. "Apparently, arranging the marriage cost him greatly, and he filed for compensation. Every time I file for housing, it is denied. He blocks it, saying I have a residence I am refusing to accept. I eat only because he ensures the food is delivered to me. Not out of kindness but to ensure that I survive to accept his offer."

My distrust melted away. Ginny was more like me than I thought. At least Blaylin had allowed me a place to live, if nothing else. She was suffering in silence and yet had put so much energy into caring for me. I walked closer and pulled her into a hug. She hugged me back, her body shaking in silent sobs.

"You can come stay with me," I insisted as she stepped back and wiped her face.

"No," she said, shaking her head. "I can't. If he found out, there's no telling what he would do. Besides, it's not so bad. I have access to the archives and books all the time."

I couldn't help the chuckle that escaped me. I had known Ginny loved the written word, and it was just like her to find that small ray of sunshine in such a dark situation.

"But won't he see that you entered that decree?" I asked, suddenly worried that I would cause her more trouble.

"Probably," she nodded. "But, I doubt he will do anything, as it was a presidential order delivered directly to me. It would mean having to go before the president and claim that I falsified it."

I let out a sigh of relief as the tone chimed through the tunnels, signaling the end of the workday. I glanced at the storage room, knowing that Ginny would be going in there as soon as I left. My heart broke for her, and Egon's words echoed in my mind once more.

"What if we ran away?" I asked, causing her eyes to go wide. "What if we just escaped to the surface and away from all this bullshit?"

She stared at me for a moment before softly shaking her head. "It's not possible," she said softly. "Others have tried, and all have failed."

Without another word, Ginny walked to the storage room and went inside. As the door clicked shut, I turned and left the archives. The tunnels were still full of people and endless chatter as I made my way to the elevator, but it was all a blur. I knew the history of the Underdark, the rules and principles on which it was founded. But it was now clear to me that those no longer applied. It was nothing but a hierarchy that forced those who were different to conform and squashed those it deemed lesser under its boot. There was no place for people like Ginny and me here, and we needed to get out and make a place for the rejects of this backward society.

Back in my room, the weight of the day threatened to crush me, but my determination remained. I would find a way for us to get out. I grabbed a piece of worn paper from the shelf and wrote a quick note to Taylor. I told him that I had a rough day and, for the first time, would not be in to work tonight. Opening my door, I let out a high-pitched whistle, and a boy came running over. He was no more than ten and too thin. I pulled a few credits from my pocket and pressed them into his hand before handing him the note.

"Taylor Riggins," I said softly.

The boy looked at the credits, more than was customary for such a task, and nodded before running down the tunnel. I did not worry that the note would find Taylor as I closed the door. I made my way to the bed and collapsed, pulling my baby blanket close to my chest. Egon's face flashed in my mind. He had cut me today, had a declaration ordered that could lead to my death, and yet, I didn't hate him. He had saved me that night, patched me up, fed me, and freed me from Blaylins' game. Not to mention that he had held onto this blanket for years, returning it to me in perfect condition.

On the exterior, he was a monster that Blaylin commanded, killing without mercy. However, that was not the side of him that I saw, that I knew. He was still the boy who took care of me when we were kids. He was still protecting me and making sure I had what I needed. Burrowing my face into the blanket let me do something I haven't done in years. I cried. Not gentle, slow tears but body-shaking sobs that I muffled with the blanket.

I had no idea how long I lay there, letting the emotions pour out of me through tears. I could feel that my face was swollen from crying, but I couldn't stop now that I had started.

A knock on the door did what I could not, and the tears instantly stopped. I forced myself up, wiping my wet face as I walked to the door. It was probably Taylor, here to make sure I was alright. I cracked open the door and felt my heart stop as I looked at my visitor, who was definitely not Taylor.

Chapter 10

I shouldn't have made her bleed. I paced my room, bare of anything except for a bed and spare uniforms. My pickaxe leaned against the stone wall, her blood still on it. I punched the wall, my own blood on the stone when I pulled back. I deserved to spill a lot more for what I did to her. Blaylin hadn't been wrong. I wasn't sure if I could have gone through with it. I had only meant to scare him into letting her go, but he had to push it further.

The only good thing to come out of it was that she was safe not only from Blaylin but from me. She had seen the monster I had become and would stay away. I looked at the pathetic excuse of a bed and flung back the pillow. There, as it had been for years, was the only piece of her I had left. I picked up the small doll. All of its limbs are different lengths, its eyes crooked, and the stuffing nearly gone.

"For you," she said as she thrust it at me. *"Now, even when we're apart, I can be with you."*

I looked at the small doll, smiling slightly. "Aren't dolls for girls?" I teased.

"Normally," she nodded, unbothered by my teasing. "But this one will keep the nightmares away. She's got superpowers."

"Then I will keep her safe forever," I grinned, clutching the doll close.

"Fuck!" I growled as I stuffed the doll in my pocket and grabbed my pickaxe.

Despite everything, I had kept that damn doll under my pillow since the day she gave it to me, and the nightmares had stopped. She had freed me from them, and in exchange, I had made myself her nightmare. I flung open the door and strode out of the manor. Everyone was asleep, and the guards on watch didn't have the guts to question me. She would be ending her shift at the speakeasy soon, and I wanted to make sure she was okay.

I normally found peace in the dark, but tonight it felt like it was trying to crush me as I pushed through it. The weight of what I had done to her pressed down harder than Blaylin's gift ever could. When I reached her tunnel, I tucked myself into the darkness and waited.

Hours crept by, and she still had not returned. Fearing something may have happened to her, I made my way to the speakeasy. The red light glowed like a beacon, and the door was locked shut. I searched around but found no signs that anything bad had happened. Slowly, I made my way to her door. There was only one way to know if she was alright. Lifting my fist, I knocked lightly on the door.

The seconds dragged by as I stood, my breath frozen in my lungs. Finally, the door slowly cracked open, and I could barely make out her silhouette in the doorway. I turned on my flashlight, shining it at the door, careful to avoid her eyes. Her face was swollen, and her eyes were red; she had been crying. On her neck, I could see the scab forming where my pickaxe had been pressed into her.

"What are you doing here?" she spoke in a hoarse voice.

"I..." The words caught in my throat, unable to explain what I was doing without pulling her back into Blaylin's sick game. Instead, I reached into my pocket and pulled out the doll. I turned it over in my hand before handing it to her. "It worked." As soon as the words left my mouth, she ripped the doll out of my hand. "I thought after today, you may need her."

She stood silent, looking at the small doll that had seen better days. I shifted on my feet, feeling uncomfortable with the silence. I could have handled her yelling at me. Hell, I would prefer it. She looked up at me, and the look on her face was not what I expected. Where there should have been fear, anger, or even disgust, there was something else. Something I hadn't seen since I was a child, compassion. Something in the still air shifted in that moment, but I did not back away. I stood like an awkward fool, soaking up every second I had with her.

Chapter 11

My heart hammered in my chest as I held the small doll that I had made years ago. I still remember the trouble I got in when it was discovered that I cut holes in my clothes to get the fabric. Of course, Blaylin thought I did it as an act of defiance to wearing the dresses he wanted. I let him believe it, fearing he would take the doll from Egon. Plus, I really didn't want to wear the dresses anyway, so he wasn't completely wrong. I looked back at him, the anger I had felt for him most of the day completely disappearing as I saw my friend once again. The big, bad Captain actually looked nervous as he began shifting on his feet. I couldn't help but let a small smile play on my lips. I opened my mouth to speak, but stopped as flashlights began moving further down the tunnel.

"I should go," Egon said, looking in the direction of the lights. "They are probably looking for me."

The lights drew closer, and I felt myself panic. I couldn't let him go, not yet. Without thinking, I grabbed the front of his shirt and pulled him inside. He stumbled in, just as surprised by my actions as I was. After locking the door, I took a few steps back and watched the door. I felt my entire body shake as I waited, expecting to hear a knock that would rip him away from me.

"What are you doing?" Egon's voice spoke behind me, making me jump.

"We're not done talking," I said, whipping around to look at him. His flashlight was still on but pointed towards the floor. The light was just enough that I could make him out in the darkness. "You don't get to do everything you've done and then disappear."

He remained still, staring at me as if I had gone insane. I took a step towards him, but stopped when his body tensed. After everything, I couldn't tell if he was afraid of himself.

"You save me, patch me up, give me food, and return my blanket," I continued. "Then, you get me promoted just to turn around and try to kill me unless I am banished from the upper levels, and now you bring me this!" My voice was louder and shaking by the time I finished and held out the doll. "Tell me the truth," I demanded. "Tell me what the hell is going on."

He stared at me for a long time, but I could see he was considering my words and deciding how to respond. His face remained hard and emotionless, but his eyes told a different story. In their deep brown depths, I could see the boy I remembered, my best friend, who I thought was gone forever.

"I can't," he finally spoke, his voice deep and gravely. I could tell that he was holding something back.

"Then why did you come here?" I spit out. "Why bring me this doll?"

He pushed past me, making his way for the door. Reaching out, I grabbed his arm, causing him to stop. His emotions immediately invaded my mind. Hurt, sorrow, regret, shame, and so many more before he ripped his arm out of my grasp.

"I'm a monster," he growled. "The person you know is gone."

"Liar," I said through clenched teeth. "A monster doesn't feel the things you do."

"I am," he yelled, running his hands over his head in frustration. "That's how everyone knows me, a reputation I have earned through years soaked in blood. But you..." His voice cut off, and he looked everywhere but at me. "I didn't want you to know, to know that I was the boy you trusted all those years ago. I never wanted you to see the monster."

I could feel the tears running down my face as he took another step towards the door. There he was, the boy I remembered. Even after everything, he was still trying to protect me, even if that meant leaving me.

"Don't," I choked out. "Don't leave me alone again."

He paused, looking over his shoulder at me. I hated the tears and the pleading sound of my voice. I didn't need anyone. I was just fine on my own, and it's how I liked it. Yet, the idea of him being out of my life again broke something inside me. It didn't matter that he had threatened to kill me or anything else he did. Some part of me needed him. It was as if a piece of me had been missing all these years, and I refused to go back to living without it.

"Damn it," he muttered, shaking his head. "You should tell me to go. That you never want to see me again."

"I can't," I admitted, stepping closer. I could feel the heat radiating off his skin without even touching him. His body was tense, but I didn't let it deter me. I would do whatever I had to do to keep him from disappearing. Egon's face slowly relaxed, and I could see the first layer of armor he surrounded himself in crack.

"He can't know," he said softly. "I'll return when I can, but you can't tell anyone."

"I promise," I said quickly. I could feel my heart hammering in my chest.

He let out a heavy sigh and opened the door with a groan. He checked the tunnel quickly before slipping out and shutting it behind him. I let out a heavy breath as I slumped onto the bed. My body shook as I allowed the tears to flow, clinging to the old doll like it was all that was keeping me from falling apart.

I didn't understand anything that was happening. My neck was still sore from where he had cut me. Yet, I clung to that doll because it was as close as I could be to him. He was right. I should hate him. Yet, all I wanted was for him to be here. He could say that he was a monster all he wanted, but I saw the real him. He could hide it from the rest of the world, but not me. I saw it in his eyes. I felt it when I touched him. He wore a mask of survival, something I understood all too well. I wore my armor every day, pretending that I feared no one and could do anything. But inside, fear and terror swirled constantly just like they had when I was a child. The only time I wasn't scared was when he was close. We had forged a bond all those years ago. I didn't know what it meant, but I knew one thing for certain: I wouldn't let him go again.

Chapter 12

Keeping last night's meeting with Egon a secret was killing me. I had always told Ginny everything freely. The way she looked at me through the stacks, I could tell she knew I was keeping a secret. She wasn't one to push, and I was thankful. I knew I would crumble under her questioning, and I couldn't break my promise the morning after making it.

Ginny had finished loading the first cart of the day, a job she did now in an attempt to keep her father from lashing out for entering the order. A job that shouldn't exist if her father would let her do her job. The president was a bastard, but at least he allowed me a place to live. Ginny and I had not talked about the previous day since I arrived. She was already here, of course, preparing the day's tasks, her normal chipper self.

Neither of us noticed the bell chiming

as someone entered. We continued on our tasks, each in our own thoughts.

"Guinevere," a stern voice spoke, shattering the silence.

My eyes shot to Ginny as she let go of the cart and walked towards the man. He was finely dressed and obviously an official. His black suit was made of fine material, showing no wear, and he wore shoes that shone even in the archive's dim light. In the lapel of the jacket was a goldrose pin. He was from Level One.

"Father," Ginny responded as she stopped in front of him, causing my jaw to drop. I had been here for over a year and had never even seen the Magistrate, let alone witnessed him come to the archives.

His face tightened as he looked at her, anger visibly boiling below the surface that he was struggling to maintain.

"You accessed the active records system yesterday," he said flatly.

"I did," Ginny nodded. "It was an urgent declaration, and I had no choice." I watched as his fists clenched, his icy gaze locked on her. I took a step forward, making my presence known. I had seen men with that look in their eyes before, just before their fist collided with a woman's face. I wanted him to know she wasn't alone and I wouldn't allow him to hurt her. He didn't even acknowledge me as his glare remained locked on Ginny.

"You made me look like a fool," he growled before his hand raised. The sound of the slap echoed through the archives, and I moved quickly. I shoved him back hard, causing him to stumble. Ginny had access to the system because of me. If he wanted to beat the person responsible, I would give him the proper target. However, if he chose to try, I would show him I wasn't so easily beaten down.

"Don't touch her!" I yelled as I pushed my way between them. "It's my fault she had to do it!"

I could feel Ginny pulling at my arm, trying to get me to leave, but I stood firm. I had had enough of people in authority throwing their weight around. This man, who denied his daughter any basic human decency, had no right to come here and lay a hand on her. He should have been begging her for forgiveness.

"Ms. Coal?" he asked, looking at me like a pest. I didn't give him words, just nodded my head. His expression was one of disgust as he wiped the wrinkles from his suit. "Guinevere, you will be taking back the responsibility of updating the records. It has been determined that it is a waste of my time for such trivial work."

"What about her earnings?" I demanded, bringing his attention back to me. "And her housing request?" We were already down the rabbit hole; I might as well see just how far it went.

"Bridgett," Ginny whispered behind me in a warning tone, but I continued to stare at the man.

"Her debt is nearly repaid," he said with disgust. "It would be impossible to find a suitable match for a woman who has expired."

My fists clenched, but he didn't seem to notice. How could a man, a father, speak about his own child in such a way? I wanted to pound his face, tell him that Ginny was so much more than some goods for him to sell as he saw fit, but I remained steady.

"Your housing assignment will be entered by the end of the day, and you will receive fifty percent of your wages," he said to Ginny. "The rest will continue to come to me as payment for the years and resources wasted on you."

With that, he turned and left as abruptly as he arrived. When I looked back at Ginny, I could see the tears running down her face.

"I'm free," she said between sobs.

I expected her to be hurt by what he called her or upset that he was still keeping half of her wages. Instead, she looked happier than I had ever seen her, lighter in a way. As much as I wanted to fight for her to get more, I decided not to sour the moment. If she was happy, then I was too.

"You deserve it," I said as I hugged her. "And so much more."

Ginny sobbed into my shoulder as she clung to me. I had never seen her break down like this before. She was always strong, determined, and sometimes so happy that it was annoying. After several minutes, her sobs stopped, and she pulled away, wiping her tears with her hands as she walked over to the terminal. I watched as she began typing, found her file, and pointed to her housing assignment. It was on level two, just a few tunnels away.

"Let's go see it," she said, turning to me.

"Let's," I nodded.

Ginny led me out of the archives and through the tunnels into the housing area. We each looked at the numbers on the units, stopping when we found hers. Ginny looked back at me over her shoulder before pressing her hand to the scanner beside the door, a security feature that wasn't wasted on those who lived in The Pit. The door slid open, revealing the home inside. Ginny walked in, covering her mouth as she looked around. The unit was furnished with a plush couch and an empty bookshelf in the main area. To the right, a kitchen area with a full countertop and sink looked brand new. Towards the back was a bedroom with a double-size bed, fresh sheets, a blanket, and pillows. Off the bedroom was a bathroom with a full-size tub. In truth, my entire apartment could have fit in the main living area. Yet I felt no jealousy. Instead, I was filled with happiness and pride for Ginny.

"We should move your things," I offered. "And then set up your credit account so you can pick up the things you are missing."

Ginny nodded, her eyes still darting around the space as if she were afraid it would disappear at any moment. She walked towards the door, stopping at the security panel inside. I watched as her fingers flew over the interface. She was obviously familiar with the technology, flying through different screens in seconds.

"Place your hand on the scanner," she instructed me.

"Ginny," I said, stepping back. "I can't."

"It's family access," she explained. "I want you to have access if you ever need it."

"Family?" I asked.

"Of course," she smiled softly. "You're like my little sister.

I stepped forward, my eyes burning with tears that I refused to let fall. I placed my hand on the scanner and waited as the machine scanned my handprint. After a few moments, it turned green, signaling that it was done.

"Finished," Ginny grinned. "Now, let's get back to work. We can take care of the other things when we finish."

I nodded and followed her back out into the tunnels. As we made our way back, I paid closer attention to the route. If Ginny needed me, I wanted to make sure I could find her place without getting lost.

Back in the archives, the rest of the day went by quickly. I brought the files to Ginny, who updated them. The process was much faster without having to deliver them. By the time the end-of-day tone sounded, we had completed what would have taken three days.

"We will finish tomorrow," Ginny grinned as she turned off the terminal.

"Ready to get moved?" I asked as I opened the storage room.

It didn't take us long, as Ginny didn't have much. We borrowed a cart and were able to take everything in one trip. At the apartment, I helped her put each item away carefully, making sure it was just how she wanted it.

"What about this?" I asked, holding up the last thing on the cart—a framed picture of a woman who looked surprisingly similar to Ginny.

"On the bookcase," Ginny smiled. "That way she can watch over me."

I placed the photo carefully. I wanted to ask her about her mother, but the question caught in my throat. She didn't seem to hate her mother as she did her father. The fact that she had the picture and wanted her mother to watch over her suggested they were close at one time. I envied that about her in a way. I had never known my mother.

"I'll return the cart," I said as I joined her. "You should head to get your credit account established. I'll meet you there."

Ginny nodded, and I saw that she was rubbing her hands. It was one of her tells when she was feeling anxious.

"Hey," I said, taking her hands in mine. "You deserve all of this."

She let out a breath as she nodded in agreement. "I'll go with you to return the cart," she said in a shaky voice. "I want you with me when I set up the account, just in case."

I nodded, and we made our way back to the archives in silence. I could feel the tension pouring off of Ginny as we walked. It was like she was waiting for everything to be ripped away from her once again. I squeezed her arm reassuringly as we walked out of the archives. She led me through the tunnels to the credits office. Just like everything else, it was a symbol of grandeur. The glass doors were spotless with large columns carved on either side. Ginny took a shaky breath before pushing them open and stepping in.

> Inside, everything was polished and pristine, with soft chairs for people to sit in while they waited. I watched as Ginny approached a woman in a fine dress and told her why she was there. The woman pointed to a chair, and I followed to sit beside Ginny. After a few moments, a man appeared and summoned her. Ginny grabbed my arm, and I followed. The man did not object as he led us back to an office and motioned for us to sit.

He didn't say a word as his fingers moved across the keys of his terminal, a clear routine he had done before.

"Half of your credits will be garnished," he said, still not looking at us. "After taxes and fees, that will leave you." He stopped speaking as he slid a piece of paper across the desk. I watched as Ginny picked it up with shaking hands and looked at me. She turned the paper towards me, and I smiled at the amount. Even as everything she was losing mounted, her credits were nearly ten times what I made.

"You deserve it," I reminded her with a whisper.

Ginny nodded as she signed the paper and slid it back to the man. He stood, still not looking at us, and walked out of the room. He returned seconds later with a metal box.

"You will be able to receive your next payment at the beginning of the month," he explained, handing it to her. "As your account is new, you are not eligible for advances for at least three years. Any questions?"

Ginny shook her head, the box firmly in her hands. The man nodded and went back to typing at his typewriter. We took this as our cue to leave, made our way out of the office, and back into the tunnels.

Ginny insisted that we stop at her apartment first so she could put most of the credits away. She didn't feel safe walking around with all of them, and I agreed. While we were there, we made a quick list of things she needed to get. I insisted that new clothes needed to be on it, and she finally agreed to two new dresses. A small victory, and if I insisted every time she got her credits, she would soon have a full wardrobe.

We headed to the shops, and I watched as Ginny made her way through the stores. She kept passing items we both agreed she needed, and I grew increasingly frustrated. After she put down the tenth bottle of soap, I had had enough. I picked up the bottle and prepared to yell at her when I caught the price tag stuck to it. I looked at it in surprise, then set it back down. Following Ginny, I saw that all the prices here were the same, more than double what I paid in the Pit just because they were in a nicer bottle.

As we walked out of the store, I could see the defeat in Ginny's face. I understood now why her credit amount was so much higher than mine. With the deductions and the prices of necessities, she wasn't making enough to afford them.

"It's not a law that you have to shop on this level," I said carefully. "We could go down to the pit and find everything you're looking for and more."

Shock spread across her face as she looked back at me. "I've never been down there," she admitted. "Would it be safe for someone like me?"

"Safer than here," I laughed. "Let me take you down. We'll get what you need, maybe have a drink, and then get you back home."

She glanced around before nodding. A big smile spread across my face as I led her towards the elevator. As the door clanged shut, I felt Ginny jump beside me. I took her hand and squeezed it. She had been stuck in the archives for so long, living in that storage room, and now she was jumping feet first into the big, bad world. I admired her bravery as the elevator quickly began its descent.

Chapter 13

As the elevator stopped, I could feel how tense Ginny was beside me. The door opened with a loud clang, and I led her off. The tunnels were relaxed as most people had headed home for the day. I led her through the winding tunnels, warning her about areas where the ground was less than smooth so she wouldn't trip. Ginny walked silently, her eyes darting around as she took in the difference between The Pit and the upper levels.

The tunnels were much shorter than they were in the upper levels. Ginny was used to tall and wide tunnels, but down here, they didn't exist. People brushed shoulders as they passed, and during peak times, we crammed in, shoulder to shoulder, to reach our destination. There were no scanners on the doors, just a lock on the inside that most of us didn't bother to use. If someone wanted to rob you, they would do it while you were gone to avoid a confrontation, since you couldn't lock the door.

When we reached the stalls, Ginny let out a gasp. I led her to each stall, watching as she looked around. She carefully chose soaps, a few dresses, a brush for her long hair, and several other things. As she paid for the items, she almost looked ashamed as she handed over the credits.

"Hello, ladies," Felix called out to us as we walked past him. "Doing a bit of shopping down in The Pit?"

"Yes," Ginny nodded nervously. My gaze flicked between her and Felix. There was something more behind her nerves than being in The Pit; I could feel it.

"Perhaps there is something I could assist you with finding?"

"No," Ginny replied firmly as she turned and led me back out of the stalls. I wanted to ask her what was going on, but held my tongue as we made our way back to my room.

I pushed open the door with its creak of metal and led her inside. I set the bags I was carrying for her on the table and turned to her with a smile. Ginny looked as if she was about to cry as she looked around my room.

"This isn't right," she finally said. "I feel like I robbed those people at the shops and now this. You helped me move into that apartment today, telling me I deserved it while you live like this."

"This is home," I shrugged. "And it was still better than the supply closet you were living in." Ginny wouldn't meet my eyes as she continued to look around. "And the people at the shops don't feel robbed," I assured her. "They have their prices set to make a profit, and any extra sales they can get means the world to them."

"It's just so different," she sighed, finally setting the bags she was holding on the table.

"Most people don't care to know," I said as I sat on the bed, leaving the chair for her. "They would rather pretend we don't exist down here."

Ginny nodded, shifting uncomfortably on her feet.

"Felix doesn't make things easier," I said casually. "But I guess you already know that."

Ginny took a shaky breath and nodded. "I've had a few encounters with him over the years."

I waited silently for her to explain. The silence was thick until Ginny finally let out a heavy breath.

"He used to come into the archives, requesting records and things I was supposed to deny him." Ginny bit her lip, shame evident on her face. "I gave in a few times; the files he requested were harmless. I finally stopped, deciding the credits he slipped me weren't worth dealing with someone like him."

Of course, Felix was known for getting information no one else could. It shouldn't have surprised me that he had tried to buy Ginny into feeding his information bank.

"No shame in it," I assured. "We've all done some shady shit for credits. Felix is a smooth talker."

"I think I could use that drink," Ginny said with a faint smile.

"Well, you will have to wait a bit longer for that," I laughed just as the power cut off. "About an hour to be more precise."

"What's going on?" Ginny gasped. I grabbed a small candle from the bedside table and struck a match. Normally, I would sit in the dark and wrap it around me like a blanket, but this was new to Ginny. I could only imagine how suffocating and terrifying the total darkness would be to her.

"Curfew," I explained as the candlelight filled the room. "Due to coal shortages, power is cut off to The Pit every night at nine and doesn't come back on until six."

"Coal shortages?" Ginny asked, confused.

"There's no shortage," I assured her. "Just a way to keep us in line. In about an hour, we'll make our way to the speakeasy, and I'll get you that drink."

"In the dark?" Ginny asked. I could hear the panic in her voice.

"Yup," I nodded. "We've got a system for finding our way around. Don't worry, I won't let you get lost."

Ginny looked around, and I could tell she was feeling anxious. "With the power off, how will I get back?"

"The elevator always has power," I explained. "People from higher up prefer the liquor of the speakeasy and sneak down here for a treat. No one will think anything of it when you leave."

Ginny nodded and picked up a book from the shelf. My small collection was all gifts from her. Yet, she looked at each as if it were new to her. I knew she was trying to be polite, so I didn't shatter the illusion.

"I still need to read the three you just gave me," I admitted. "Things are just crazy, right now."

"That's an understatement," Ginny laughed.

The rest of the hour passed by in cheerful conversation. It felt strange having someone to talk to like this, but I liked it. When it was time, I opened the door and took Ginny's hand. She held on tight as I led her down the dark tunnel, following the line carved into the wall. The red light of the speakeasy came into view, and I felt her grip relax.

Inside, Taylor was already behind the bar, setting up. He glanced up at me, and I could see that he was nearly healed from the attack. The bruises were now a pale yellow, and the swelling was gone. He didn't seem phased that I had Ginny with me.

"Can my friend get a drink?" I smiled as I walked closer. "She's celebrating."

"Of course," Taylor nodded with a grin as he set three glasses on the bar and filled them with the clear liquor.

I took two and handed one to Ginny. We toasted with Taylor and drank. I couldn't help but laugh at the face Ginny made as she lowered the glass from her lips.

"Delicious," she coughed as she placed a hand on her chest.

"It gets better the more you drink," Taylor laughed as he refilled her glass.

"Not too much," I warned him. "We don't need her passing out in the elevator."

Taylor shooed me away with his hand, and I moved to preparing the tables and turning on the music. I returned to the bar just as people started to file in. I set about serving drinks and enjoying how normal the night felt. After the events of the night before Assignment Day, normal was just what I needed.

The speakeasy was full of people laughing and blowing off steam. I weaved between the tables, delivering drinks and taking orders with ease. The faces all blurred together as I moved around, taking little notice of whom I was serving.

"Surprised to see you're still moonlighting as a waitress." A deep voice stopped me in my tracks.

I looked back at the patron I just served and saw him. Egon was sitting at the table as if he frequented here. My breath caught in my throat as I leaned closer to him.

"What are you doing here?" I asked in a hushed tone. I wasn't sure he could hear me over the music and conversations that filled the cavern.

"You demanded to see me again," he replied with a raised eyebrow. "I went to your room, but you weren't there."

I looked around, worried that someone might be watching us. Egon had been clear that no one could know we were talking. It was surprising that he was speaking to me in such a public place. However, the other patrons were too absorbed in their own conversations to notice us.

"We're open for another hour," I replied. "Then I'll lead Ginny to the elevator and go home."

Egon followed my gaze as I looked over at Ginny, who was laughing at something Taylor said at the bar. For the first time, I noticed how friendly they seemed, given that they had just met. I couldn't be sure, or maybe I was in denial, but it looked like they were flirting.

"I heard about that," Egon replied, pulling my attention back to him. "I will wait and escort you both."

I wanted to argue, but shouts for drinks began to ring out. Not wanting to draw attention to us, I set to work again. As the hour ticked by, I could feel his eyes on me as I moved. The weight of the gaze made me move less expertly, tripping over chair legs and nearly spilling my tray several times. I breathed a sigh of relief as the last patron left, Egon following them out.

"I'll clean up," Taylor called to me. "I think Ms. Ginny here is ready for bed."

I made my way over to the bar and could see that poor Ginny was starting to fall asleep on the stool.

"How much did she drink?" I asked, placing my hand on her shoulder.

"Not half the limit," Taylor smirked. "Still, I think it was enough to free her of a weight she carried. Now, she needs rest. She is welcome here any time."

Ginny looked up at me with a sleepy smile. I helped her to her feet and led her out. Once we stepped into the glow of the red light, I spotted Egon waiting. He wrapped an arm around Ginny, helping me guide her through the tunnels. When we reached the branch for the elevator, Egon shifted all of Ginny's weight to him.

"I'll take her to her apartment," Egon's voice cut through the darkness.

"You don't know where she lives," I quipped. "I got her."

I tried to shift Ginny's weight to me, but Egon held firm. "I know where to take her," he said firmly. "Now go back to your room and wait for me there."

I opened my mouth to argue, but Ginny's weight completely disappeared as he walked away. I heard his boots walk off into the darkness as I followed the line back to my room. Once inside, I let out a long sigh. I had hoped that he would come back with me, but I couldn't argue with him helping Ginny. I quickly changed out of the jumpsuit and put on a fresh shirt and panties before sinking into the bed. I accepted that he wouldn't be back tonight.

He had already spent too much time waiting for me tonight.

The dark felt suffocating as I lay there unable to sleep. I sat up with a huff and relit the candle. I immediately noticed that all of Ginny's things were still there. I would have to deliver them to her in the morning. I grabbed a book and settled close to the candle. I opened Dracula and started slowly making my way through the pages. A knock on my door caused me to jump, dropping the book to the ground.

Scolding myself, I picked it up and placed it on the table. I had become jumpy in recent days, a weakness that I was not fond of. I would need to work harder to shed it. Cracking open the door, I was surprised to find Egon standing outside.

"May I come in?" he asked after a long, awkward silence had passed.

I nodded, stepping back and then shutting the door behind him. When I turned back around, I felt my cheeks flush. Egon's eyes were wide as they raked over my body. I had forgotten that I was wearing very little.

"Sorry," I said as I tried to rush past him to get a jumpsuit.

"Don't," Egon said in a guttural tone. "This is your home. I want you to be comfortable."

Comfortable wasn't the word I would use, but I nodded. I sat on the bed as he sat in the chair. His body was rigid, his hands clenched on his thighs. His eyes remained locked on me, their deep brown showing in the candlelight.

"I didn't know you would be coming back," I said, shattering the silence.

"Your friend, Ginny, insisted I did," he replied. "I assured her I had every intention of doing so."

I picked at the edge of my shirt, a new nervous tic that I immediately hated. Why did he have this effect on me? I flattened out the fabric and took a deep breath.

"I'm glad you did," I said in a voice that came out stronger than I felt. "I still have so many questions."

Egon didn't move; his brown eyes remained fixed on me.

"Why is it so important that Blaylin never learn we are talking?" I asked.

The silence stretched, and I feared he would refuse to answer.

"He would take it as a victory," Egon replied, his posture still rigid.

His answer gave me no answers.

"What does that mean?" My nerves were fried, and my frustration was bursting forth.

"You don't need to worry about it," Egon said flatly. "I have taken care of it."

That was all I could take. My anger took over as I smacked my mattress in frustration. "You can't protect me!" I said loudly. "I am part of this game, and I'm at a disadvantage. I don't know what the damn game is!"

In the dim candlelight, I could have sworn I saw something akin to shame and hurt flash in his eyes. He adjusted in the chair and went rigid once more.

"He didn't take either of us in out of charity or duty," Egon began. "You remember our lessons, the president's title passing down through generations of the same bloodline since the first one was elected?"

"I do," I nodded. "But Blaylin has no children."

"No, he doesn't," Egon nodded. "He had hoped to raise me as his successor, but a law stating that the president must be born in Underdark prevented it. Your arrival was what he needed. He was grooming us to give him a child he could raise as his successor. He needed us both to be compliant and devoted to him for it to be successful."

"But I refused to be either." The realization washed over me as I spoke.

"He sent you here hoping to break you, but failed," Egon continued. "His time is running out, and he has decided to change the plan. He was going to order me to force myself upon you to conceive a child, taking it at birth, and claim that you died."

"That sick bastard!" I said through gritted teeth. I looked at Egon and noticed he was holding his hands up in surrender. I had unconsciously pushed myself further onto the bed, away from him. "Sorry," I breathed. "I know you wouldn't."

"Do you?" Egon asked as he lowered his hands. "It is just another reason for you to tell me to stay away from you."

"No," I said, shaking my head. "You saved me that night."

"Perhaps because I wanted you for myself."

"You could have forced yourself on me then," I replied. "Instead, you took care of me, careful not to touch me."

"To protect my emotions."

"Until last night," I retorted. "You had no desire to do so."

I watched as Egon searched his mind for another argument, but silence stretched. He did not argue, and his shoulders relaxed slightly as he accepted his defeat.

"I win," I smiled

"As always," Egon nodded.

A simple moment. No deep revelations. No intense feelings. Just two souls enjoying each other, just like we had when we were young. It came naturally, as if no time had passed. Egon relaxed, and I caught him trying to stifle a yawn.

"Sleepy?" I teased.

"A bit," he nodded. "I didn't have my friend to keep the nightmares away."

I reached over and picked up the small doll from where it rested beside my pillow.

"You take her tonight," I said, holding out the doll. "I'll take her tomorrow."

"Are you guaranteeing I will come back?" Egon asked as he took the doll.

"Maybe," I shrugged. My emotions screamed inside me. Yes, I wanted him to come back and not just to talk. For years, I became as rough and rugged as a callus. However, whenever I was around Egon, I felt my defenses disappear and my softer side come to the surface. It both excited and terrified me.

Chapter 14

Ginny was a mess the next morning. I had entered her apartment an hour before we were supposed to be at the archives. She was still in bed, passed out, wearing the same clothes she had worn the night before.

"Rise and shine," I said in my most chipper voice.

Ginny let out a grumble as she slowly began to stir. Holding one hand on her head, she slowly emerged from the bed and looked at me. I knew I shouldn't laugh at my friend's suffering, but I couldn't help the light giggle that escaped me.

"Shut up," she growled as she threw a pillow at me, missing me.

"You jump in the shower," I laughed. "I'll make you some breakfast, and then it's off to work."

"Shower?" she asked, her voice tinged with panic. "My stuff I..."

"I brought it all," I assured her. "Everything is on the table. Now, get moving before you make us both late."

I went to the kitchen and heard her shuffling behind me. I set out to make her a quick breakfast while she grabbed her shower supplies and disappeared into the bathroom. I had just set the plate on the counter when she emerged in fresh clothes, her hair still slightly damp. She slumped into the chair and slowly took a bite.

"I doubt we'll be finishing those record updates today," I teased.

"We will," Ginny said, not looking at me. "I just need my head to stop throbbing, and the rest will be easy."

"It's no big deal if it takes us three days instead of two," I assured her. "That's still weeks faster than it has been in years."

Ginny took another bite and gently shook her head in agreement. I wasn't sure whether she actually agreed or whether she lacked the strength to argue further. I waited in silence as she forced herself to finish her breakfast, impressed that she managed to keep it all down, and then we left for the archives together. I didn't talk, trying to allow her head a chance to rid itself of the headache I could tell was pounding in her skull. She had taken a double dose of headache powder before we left, but it would still be a while before she felt relief.

"You sit and rest your head," I insisted once we were in the archives. "I'll go load up the first cart."

Ginny didn't answer but made her way to the desk. Her head was down with her eyes closed as I looked back over my shoulder. I took my time loading the cart, wanting to give her as much time as possible. When I finished, I stood leaning against the shelves, thinking about the night before. Everything was getting more complicated every time we were together. He was bringing out a weakness in me, and I could see that I was having the same effect on him. If we continued, whatever this was, it would put us both in danger. Yet, I couldn't bring myself to stop seeing him. The thought of losing him again caused a pain in my chest that I hadn't felt before.

"Bridgett!" Ginny's voice echoed through the stacks.

I grabbed the cart, pushing all thoughts of Egon from my mind, and made my way back to the front. Ginny wasted no time upon my arrival and began updating the files. Her pace was only slightly slower than it was the day before. I waited while she worked, wanting to take the cart and refill it to give her a break in between loads.

When she finished, she lay her head back on the counter and closed her eyes. I returned to the stacks, placing the files back and getting the next load. When I returned, she was upright once more, looking less like a zombie as she began to work.

"Poor soul," Ginny said to herself as she closed a file and returned it to the cart. She immediately grabbed another file and set to work, as if she hadn't realized she had spoken out loud.

"What's wrong?" I pried, eager for something to stimulate my mind.

"Just a discovered gift," Ginny said, shaking her head. "Poor child lost control and exposed herself. She's in for a long, hard life."

That was the rule of the Underdark. Everyone who had gifts kept them to themselves, especially those of poorer families. A gift, if deemed powerful or desirable, was either a life of servitude or a death sentence. We were taught to keep them a secret, even to make up deformities if pressed. It was just another thing we had to do to survive.

The only person who knew about my gift was Egon. I had never let anyone else know that secret. He still hadn't discovered his when we were separated, so I had no idea. In fact, I still had no clue what Ginny's gift was either. Sometimes, if you studied a person long enough, you could find clues in the way they did things. I watched Ginny as she worked, typing, printing, adding to the file, and moving on to the next. If she had a gift, she had perfected hiding it.

"Couldn't figure it out?" Ginny asked as she returned the last file to the cart.

I blinked in surprise as I shifted uncomfortably. I didn't want to lie to her, but it was a question that everyone knew not to ask.

"Sorry," I said, quickly taking the cart. "I shouldn't have tried. It's not something we are supposed to share."

"Everyone tries to figure it out anyway," Ginny smiled. "For example, I know you do not like skin-to-skin contact. If I had to guess, it's probably because you absorb something from people when you touch. Probably, memories or emotions?"

My jaw fell open. I thought I was good at hiding my ability, but Ginny had figured it out, almost exactly.

"Emotions," I answered with a shaky voice.

Ginny nodded and leaned against the desk. "Mine isn't so easy to see, but it only seems fair to share it now."

"You don't have to," I insisted.

Ginny held up her hand, signaling me to stop.

"It's nothing grand," she assured me. "In fact, it's one of the many reasons I am such a disappointment to my father. I have loved books since I was a child, and my gift appeared almost as soon as I learned how to read. When I read, I can project the image and watch the story unfold. My father tried for years to help me expand it, to project things that could be useful. He believes he failed, but in truth, I refused."

"You'll have to show me that sometime," I smiled.

"I will," she agreed. "But for now, we should focus on finishing these damn files.

I nodded and pushed the cart away. I stopped and turned back to Ginny. "The girl," I started. "What was her gift?"

"Electrical currents," Ginny sighed. "Both external and internal. The poor girl will either be used as a battery or forced to kill for the rest of her life. Not something I would wish on anyone, especially someone who's six years old."

I nodded and slowly made my way back into the stacks. Ginny was right; that poor girl would live out the rest of her life as those in charge deemed fit. Knowing Blaylin the way I did, it would be most likely that she would be forced to kill.

Chapter 15

What is happening to me!? In just a week, Bridgett has turned my life upside down and twisted me inside out. I thought compassion was something I was no longer capable of. I had to let it go to be what Blaylin wanted, but since that night in the tunnels, things are different. It was her death that allowed me to shut it down. Without her, I didn't care about anyone or anything. Now that she's back, everything is different. No matter how hard I try, I can't stay away from her. I know it's not safe, not with Blaylin watching. In his eyes, he would be getting what he always wanted.

Still, I can't help but consider the possibility that maybe Bridgett and I could make this work. I would rather have her in secret than not at all. What remains unseen is whether she will still want me once she knows everything. She didn't flinch at what I had done, the people I killed. She found a way to show that I wasn't the monster I saw myself as. My gift was something else entirely. I hid it well, even from Blaylin. If he knew what I could do, people would be killed in such great numbers that I would lose myself completely. It was the gift of a monster, meant for death and destruction.

I stopped in the small room. It felt like it was closing in on me as I stood in the center of it, raking my hands through my hair. This woman was going to kill me. I listened as the sounds of the manor slowly slipped away, signaling that Blaylin and the staff had retired for the night. It was time. Moving quickly through the halls, I was out and to the elevator in a matter of minutes.

"Going down?"

Ginny stood there with a sly smile as soon as the elevator stopped. The heavy door slammed open, and she stepped inside. I was surprised to see her going back, especially after last night.

"Just one drink tonight," she said with a smile as if she could read my mind. "I am mainly going for the company. It's a nice place to relax."

I nodded, words refusing to form as the elevator descended. My mind raced with what I would say to Bridgett. How could I explain my gift without sounding like a horrible person? Images of her reacting in the worst ways flashed through my mind. By the time the elevator stopped, I felt as if I might be sick.

I followed Ginny out, and we walked in silence through the darkness to the speakeasy. As soon as we arrived, Ginny made her way to the bar without even glancing at me. My eyes searched the cavern, not stopping until I spotted her. Even from a distance, her presence was more intoxicating than the moonshine. I watched as she made her way through the tables, smiling at each person as she served drinks. Occasionally, I could tell she was talking to them, but the music drowned out her words.

After several minutes, her eyes found mine. I watched as a faint flush appeared on her face before she looked away and went back to work. Her movements weren't as graceful as before. Perhaps I had the same effect on her that she had on me. I made my way to an empty table and sat down. She arrived a few moments later and sat with a smirk in front of me.

"Two nights in a row," she smiled. "Does this mean you are becoming a regular?"

I picked up the glass and slowly sipped the clear liquid. "Maybe," I said, setting my glass back down. "There is something to be said about the atmosphere."

She nodded and quickly walked off. I continued to take small sips of the moonshine, my eyes locked on her as she worked. As everyone began to leave, I was glad to see Ginny had kept her word and was walking just fine on her own. She smiled at me as she headed out. Taylor spotted me and whispered something to Bridgett. I watched her seem to assure him and usher him towards the door.

"Everything alright?" I asked once we were alone.

"Of course," she smiled back. "He just worries about me since..."

Her voice cut off, and I could tell she was still holding pain from the night she was almost raped. She turned and began stacking the glasses, wiping tables, and putting up the chairs. I moved and began helping, working my way across the cavern until I met with her.

"All done," she chimed as the last chair was slid onto the table. "Just let me turn off the music, and we can head out."

I walked closer to the exit, waiting as silence filled the cavern, and she joined me. The tension was thick in the air as we walked out, and she locked the door. I watched as she placed her hand on the wall and began to follow the trail through the dark. I followed behind her, watching her as she moved. It was obvious she had made this trip more times than could be counted. Her feet seemed to know where every bump and hurdle was, stepping over them with grace.

When we reached her room, I followed her inside, watching as she found a candle and brought a dim light into the small room. She took the same position as the night before on her bed, and I sat in the chair. It creaked under my weight but seemed steady enough to hold. That's what I needed, the damn chair collapsing under me while I made my confession. "You've got something on your mind," she said, forcing me to look at her. It wasn't a question but a statement—an accurate one at that.

"Always," I said flatly. I could feel myself losing my nerve to tell her. Maybe she didn't need to know for this to work.

"I'm waiting," she pressed, leaning towards me.

This damn woman. She wouldn't let this go, and I knew I had no choice. I could either tell her and let it play out or keep the secret and lose her. Either option was shit, but only one had a slim chance of keeping her.

"You're gift," I said, looking at her. "Does it ever scare you?"

"No," she said quickly. "I hate it, but it doesn't scare me. I've learned to live with it. I can't imagine being scared of someone's gift. Even with as terrible as Blaylin is, I do not fear his gift. He chooses to use it for harm."

I nodded at her words and let the silence settle in around us. It stretched on, but I couldn't bring myself to continue.

"Are you afraid of yours?" she asked, causing me to wince slightly.

"I'm afraid of what it could be used for if discovered," I admitted with a sigh.

"Understandable. Does it have something to do with why you don't need to use the guidelines in the dark?"

I looked at her with surprise. How could she possibly know that?

"I figured it out the night we bumped into each other," she explained. "Though I don't think I fully realized it until tonight. You grabbed me with one hand and held the flashlight in the other when you dragged me through the tunnels. Unless you have a third hand, I haven't noticed, you had to be able to see in some way."

"Blood," I answered. "I can focus and see blood, illuminating it so I can seek it out. The tunnels are covered in it, especially down here."

She let out a laugh. "You're afraid that you can make blood glow but only for yourself?"

"That's how it started," I replied, my mouth going dry. "I can't just make it illuminate so I can see, I can do things to it."

"What kinds of things?"

I expected to hear fear in her voice, but there was only genuine curiosity. How I wish I didn't have to continue, but she deserved to know.

"Boil, freeze, leave the body, flow the wrong direction," I said, naming a few. "Anything I want. Sometimes I use it to show mercy to those I am ordered to execute. Freezing someone's blood stops the heart and makes their death painless. The others, I use them on those who deserve to suffer before they die."

The silence settled back in like a heavy blanket as soon as I finished talking. I waited, allowing her to absorb the information and tell me to get the fuck away from her. It's what any sane person would do. But Bridgett was not known for being sane.

Chapter 16

"Why haven't you made that bastard, Blaylin, bleed out in his sleep?"

The words burst out of me, and I could see the shock and confusion on Egon's face. Obviously, my reaction was not what he expected.

"It's not that simple," he replied after a moment. "Killing him wouldn't fix the issue. It would just put someone else in control, someone who could be worse than him."

I shook my head, frustration burning inside me. No one could be worse than Blaylin. If anyone was, this world was fucked beyond repair.

"You're afraid of him," I said, anger dripping in my words. "You have the power to stop him, but you're too scared."

Egon stood so fast that the chair hit

the floor. I felt myself jump, but kept my gaze locked on him.

"No," he growled, leaning close to my face. "I'm trying to do what I thought you wanted: protect as many people as I can. His death would make things worse. I've heard him be scolded like a child for being too soft on the people here. Threats that if an heir is not conceived, a person from outside the Underdark will be sent to rule, as he has proven incapable of doing! Do you know how many people would die?! I would be the one sentencing them to death just for revenge!"

"Scolded by who?" I asked, my voice shaking despite myself.

"Like I fucking know?!" Egon continued to yell. "A voice, a man's. The calls happen once a month like clockwork, and no one is allowed in the room. Whoever it is, even Blaylin fucking fears him!"

My chest hurt as I looked at the anger and hurt in his eyes. I knew he hated Blaylin as much as I did, and I accused him of being too afraid to stand up to him. As crappy as it was, I had still managed to get free of Blaylin. Egon had been forced to stand by and watch, learning secrets and things that I had no access to. For the first time, I felt like I had betrayed him by doubting his motives.

He had started this by talking about fearing gifts. It was obvious that he told me about his situation to give me a chance to make a clean break. Instead, I used it against him and hurt him.

"Tell me to leave," he said with heavy breaths. "Tell me you never want to see me again."

"Why would I do that?" It was my turn to be confused.

He moved quickly, his hand moved up the back of my neck, gripping my hair and pulling me off the bed. My body was pressed firmly against his, and I could feel the confused emotions radiating off him. I tried to block them out and focused on his face.

"I can't do it," he said in a deep voice. "I can't walk away from you. Not unless you tell me to go."

"And if I don't?" I asked as I leaned closer against him. "What if I want you to stay?"

"Then there's no going back." I could feel the words vibrate through his chest, the blocked emotions begging me to pay attention. "After tonight, you will be mine."

I felt my core clench at his words and a wetness begin to gather between my thighs. The idea of being his was enough to push me over the edge. Yet, there was something more I wanted. Something more I needed.

"After tonight, you'll be mine," I replied, looking into his dark brown eyes.

Immediately, something ignited with him, and whatever had been keeping us separated was gone. He pulled my face to his, and his mouth pressed greedily over mine. Tilting my head back, I pulled him closer, deepening the kiss. The heat from his body enveloped me, and I could feel the tension in him as he devoured my mouth with his own; he was holding back.

I had escaped, all be it in a shitty way, and been in control of my own life for

years. He had been trapped and used, never knowing how it felt to be in control. He needed it, and I wanted to be the one to give it to him. As much as he needed to be the one in control, I needed someone to take control. I didn't, couldn't, trust anyone else except for him—something in the fabric of my very being demanded as my entire body pulsed at his touch.

His free hand began to roam down my side, his thick, calloused hands scraping me through my thin shirt, while his other hand remained firm, holding my short hair. I let him take control, deciding how fast and how far this would go. It both terrified and excited me.

Slowly, his hand made it to the sleeves of my jumpsuit tied around my waist. His grip on my hair tightened as he let out a low growl and broke the kiss. I stared at him, my chest falling and rising with heavy breaths.

"Last chance," he said through clenched teeth.

"I'm yours," I said without question, pressing myself against him. I could feel his length through his pants and knew that stopping now would hurt him just as much as it would me. He moved quickly, like an animal released from its cage. Before I could react, my jumpsuit was untied and lying on the floor around my feet. I hadn't even noticed him move before my feet left the floor, and he lay me roughly on the bed.

The flicker of candlelight illuminated him just enough for me to see him standing above me. He pulled his shirt over his head with one arm, dropping it to the floor. My eyes trailed down his bare chest, soaking up each chiseled feature. Just as my eyes reached his waist, he undid his belt and let his pants fall away. I gulped as I took in all of him in front of me. I wasn't sure if the perfect man existed before this moment. Now that I had him, I sure as hell wasn't going to let him go.

I pulled at my shirt, tossing it to the floor, leaving myself in just panties as he bent over me. My body buzzed as he crawled up the bed, nipping at my flesh as he moved. When he reached my panties, he looked up at me with those dark eyes. I could see the hunger and desire, but also the question, one I was growing tired of answering. I thrust myself towards him and watched as his entire body tensed. In one swift movement, he pulled my panties with his teeth and tore them away, leaving me completely bare.

My body tensed as his hands slowly explored my exposed flesh. I felt myself shudder under his touch as the heat continued to grow inside me.

"I'm not your first," he said as his fingers slowly circled my nipples. It wasn't a question but a statement. "But after tonight, I will be the only one you remember."

I felt my core clench at his words as he quickly pulled my hardened nipple into his mouth. Pleasure exploded through me as I gripped onto him, already a moaning mess just from the little touch he had given me. He released my nipple and gave it a nip with his teeth that caused me to gasp before moving on to the next. I could feel his length brushing against my core, and my body was already begging for more.

He released my nipple in the same way, and I swore he was smiling when I gasped. His hand slid down my body and began to feel at my center. "So wet for me," he growled. Words refused to form as his fingers found my clit and began to rub it in tight circles. My back arched off the bed as the feeling consumed me. I could feel that I was already building towards an orgasm, nearly ready to crash over the edge just as he stopped.

I lay there panting, my body begging for the release it was denied, but my brain was unable to form the words.

"Not without me," he said firmly as he positioned himself at my entrance. "You don't get to come without me."

He slammed into me, roughly and without warning. I felt myself stretch around his length, my body instantly reacting to the sudden fullness. He didn't give me time to adjust before he pulled out and thrust into me again. I gripped his arms, desperate for something to anchor myself to before I completely disappeared into a sea of ecstasy. I felt him shift as his thrusts picked up speed, and his fingers were once again on my clit. My back arched, and I felt the orgasm rushing to the surface. I looked at him, my eyes begging for permission that I couldn't vocalize. "Come for me," he replied, his speed intensifying. "Be a good girl and come for me."

That was it. My orgasm ripped through my body, causing my entire body to tremble as my core squeezed around his length. I screamed into the darkness, the only sound I was able to make. A few thrusts later, he let out a growling cry that signaled he had reached his own release. His pace slowed as he worked me through my orgasm before lying down beside me.

For a while, the only sound was our labored breathing, the light dwindling as the candle was nearly spent. As our breathing began to slow, Egon grabbed me by the waist and pulled my back against him. His grip on me felt both safe and possessive, and I loved it.

"Mine," he breathed into my ear.

"Mine," I whispered back, clenching his hand at my waist.

Chapter 17

Everything felt perfect for the first time I could remember. I floated through the archives, completing the list of tasks that Ginny had given me when I arrived. My bed had been empty when I woke up, but I could still feel the heat of his presence. It hadn't been my first time, but last night was different. I never allowed myself to feel his emotions, and yet it was the most connected I had ever felt with someone. I hated being away from him and knew that our time together would be limited and secret, but I didn't care. Every moment I get to spend with Egon is one that I would treasure.

"You're in a good mood today," Ginny grinned as she appeared behind me.

Of course, I was in a good mood. I finally found what I had been missing, not that I could tell her that. I trusted Ginny with my life, but this wasn't just my secret. Egon had been clear that no one could know about our relationship. Though I was sure that Ginny had already put together that something was going on, it wasn't my place to admit it. I hated keeping it a secret from her, but what choice did I have?

"Slept well last night." Not a lie, but not the complete truth either.

Ginny raised a knowing eyebrow at me but didn't push. It didn't stop the knot from forming in my stomach from not being honest. Still, I kept smiling as I worked, removing a few more books from the shelves slated for destruction. These were not like the ones Ginny had given me. Their spines were broken to the point that pages were falling out. Not that it mattered if a few were lost, the writing was so faded that I couldn't make out any of the words.

It surprised me that these had made it so long. The ones I had were in much better condition and were scheduled for destruction. Whatever the process was for determining which books to destroy and which to repair, it had a flaw. At least the materials would not be wasted. While most waste was burned in the incinerator, the books would not be so treated. The paper would be recycled and used in new works. It was sad, but beautiful at the same time. "Are you working again tonight?"

Ginny's question caught me by surprise. Of course, I was working tonight, but she had never questioned my schedule before. Something in her voice made it seem like she was almost nervous to ask.

"Yup," I nodded. "You coming down again?"

"I think so," Ginny nodded.

Ginny tried to look away, but I still noticed the blush on her cheeks. I had seen her at the bar for the last few nights. I thought back and remembered that it looked almost as if she and Taylor had been flirting. Taylor was a good man and a father figure to me. He took on the role well, seeing as he had three daughters he was raising alone. I still didn't know how he managed to do it. The girls were fifteen, twelve, and six, and he was their reason for everything. His wife had died giving birth to the youngest, and it nearly destroyed him. Yet, he kept going for those girls. He ran the speakeasy not only to make ends meet but also to ensure he could continue to provide for his girls, so they would never know a struggle like mine.

    I had met them all a few times over the years. I remember the eldest, Miranda, was particularly upset when she first met me. At first, I had thought she believed I was trying to become her new stepmother. Laughable since I was still a child myself. The reality was that she was upset that Taylor was allowing me to work at the speakeasy and refused to let her. She wanted to help, but he refused, stating she would never need to worry about such things.

    I hoped that if Ginny was interested in Taylor, she was ready for the three lives he would bring into her life. Taylor's girls would always be his priority. A fact that many women couldn't handle. I had seen him date several times, each one ending when he refused to compromise on his children. Most women want to be the center of their man's world and build their own family. Few would accept his daughters into their family, and most wanted to send them away for a fresh start.

"You and Taylor seemed to hit it off," I said as I raised my eyebrow at her.

Ginny's cheeks immediately flushed a dark crimson as she tried to look away. "He's an amazing man," she finally said. "The way he is dedicated to his children, despite everything it costs him. Those girls are lucky to have a father willing to sacrifice so much for them."

I immediately flashed back to seeing Ginny interacting with her own father. He had thrown her away without a second thought for not living up to his expectations. Of course, she would admire a man like Taylor, who would not give up on his children. Perhaps she was the perfect match for him.

"They are," I nodded. "Though I think Taylor needs to recognize that he needs to prepare them for more and stop shielding them from everything."

"Like what?" Ginny asked, facing me with a look of concern.

"I know Meridith and Gladis want to help out at the speakeasy, learn to run it one day for when Taylor no longer can," I explained. "But he is so determined that they will not need to do that; he won't let them set foot in there."

Ginny nodded knowingly, "You're worried they won't be ready for the day he's no longer there to provide for them."

"It will happen one day," I sighed. "I just don't want them to struggle as I did."

"Nor do I," Ginny agreed. "Maybe together we can help him see that."

I couldn't help but laugh. "You've got a better chance than I. I'm pretty sure I'm his unofficial fourth daughter."

Ginny smiled as she nodded in agreement. We both kept working, finishing our tasks with ease. As the tone sounded, signaling the end of the day, Ginny followed me to the doors.

"Bridgett." Ginny grabbed my arm, keeping me from opening the door and stepping out. "Have you had a chance to read any more of those books?"

I looked at her blankly for a moment. There was something behind her question, but I couldn't figure out what it was. "I started another," I replied. "Dracula."

"Good," Ginny sighed. "Just remember, books do more than tell a story. There is often something deeper hidden in the pages."

"I know," I said, rolling my eyes. "There's some type of lesson there if you are willing to see it."

"Especially with those books," Ginny said, ignoring my sarcasm. "You make sure to pay CLOSE attention."

With that, Ginny pushed past me and opened the door. I watched her go, confusion washing over me. Ginny had always been a bit odd, but this was weird even for her. I walked out the door, determined to ask her what she meant, but she was already lost in the sea of people. It didn't matter; I would see her tonight. I turned and headed for the elevator. I would go home and read more of my book. It would help pass the time until the speakeasy was open.

Chapter 18

"Another round!"

I sighed as I carried my tray over to a group of miners who had pushed a couple of the tables together. They hadn't said much, except for ordering more rounds since they arrived. However, their faces told me that something had happened today.

"Only one more and you are at the limit," I said as I set the glasses down.

"Fuck the limit," the older one who had ordered the round huffed. "You will keep bringing them until we either say we've had enough or drink ourselves to death."

I could see they were dealing with something, but my anger still rose like bile in the back of my throat. "Not an option," I said as I set the last glass down. "Rules are rules. Going over the limit makes you a danger to this place."

The man's hand slammed down on the table, but it didn't rattle me. Tucking my now-empty tray under my arm, I looked back at him sternly. "Throwing a fit won't change things."

I barely registered the scrape of the chair on the floor as he stood up and his giant, calloused hand reached for me. Before I could react, someone grabbed his wrist and twisted his arm away. I looked to see Egon standing there, rage burning in his eyes.

"No touching," Egon growled, twisting the man's arm and causing him to let out a cry of pain. None of the other miners moved. They all looked at Egon as if he were death come for them.

"That's enough," I said, placing my hand on Egon's arm. "They have obviously had a rough day, and I'm sure he didn't mean any harm."

Egon looked at me as he twisted the man's arms once more and finally let him go. The man fell back into his chair, clutching his arm. Egan grabbed my wrist and led me away to the bar. I didn't fight; I needed to go there anyway for more drinks. At least that's what I told myself.

Egon made his way straight to where Taylor was talking with Ginny. The smile immediately disappeared from Taylor's face as soon as we arrived.

"Problem?" Taylor asked, looking at me.

"No," I said, pulling my wrist free from Egon. "Just some miners upset about the limit."

"You should let them drink their fill," Egon said in a rough voice. "Perhaps just put a few jars on the table to allow them to help themselves so they don't get any ideas about touching again."

Taylor looked surprised for a second but quickly recovered. "We have a limit for a reason," he said, shaking his head. "More than that, people get stupid and put us all at risk."

Egon looked back at the miners and then at Taylor. "They are more of a risk sober," he said softly. "There was a collapse today in Mine Sixteen."

Ginny let out a gasp and covered her mouth.

"How bad?" Taylor asked, already reaching for jars.

"Over two hundred men were working there," Egon explained. "Those are all that made it out."

I looked back at the tables, and the thirteen miners gathered around them. They were all that survived. They had lost so many brothers today; no wonder they were in such a state.

"Wait," I said, turning back to Egon. "There was no announcement."

Normally, an accident such as a collapse was announced throughout the Underdark. However, there hadn't been anything today.

"The President has ordered it to remain silent," Egon said, looking at me with hard eyes. "Those men have been ordered to silence. Failure to do so will lead to not only their lives being forfeit but the lives of all the surviving family members of the lost miners."

"Shit!" I could tell there was more to the story, but something in Egon's stare told me not to push, not here. That could only mean one thing: Blaylin was up to something and wanted to keep it secret.

Taylor set several jars of shine on the bar. I reached to grab them, but Egon stepped in my way. "I'll take it," he said as he gathered up the jars. "There are others who are still waiting on their drinks."

I set my tray on the counter and waited for Taylor to fill it up with fresh glasses. I watched as Egon took the jars over to the miners and set them down on the table. Then, to my surprise, he placed a hand on the older miner's shoulder and said something I couldn't hear. The man pounded his fist on his chest, and Egon nodded back. I knew the action, a sign of respect among miners. I had nearly forgotten that Egon had spent time in the mines, had become one of them—a symbol he still carried with his pickaxe.

Pickaxe. Where was his pickaxe? I was grateful he didn't have it earlier; otherwise, the older man might have felt his full wrath. I looked around and spotted it behind the bar.

"You took it?" I looked at Taylor.

"No weapons allowed," Taylor nodded. "Told him the other night that if he brought it, it would have to stay here. Make sure he takes it tonight. I don't need him knocking on my door before the lights are on for me let him in to get it."

I nodded as I picked up my tray and set back to work. Egon stayed at the miners' table. I could feel him watching me as he sat with them. At least he would be there if the shine took a turn and any of them got out of control.

The rest of the night went on without incident. The miners were the last to leave, but they each gave me a nod as they slowly walked towards the exit. I was surprised to see that Ginny was still seated at the bar, sipping on a glass of shine. It looked to be the same one she ordered when she arrived.

I set to cleaning up, noticing that Egon was helping me once again. Soon, everything was clean, and it was time to head out.

"We need to talk," Taylor's voice boomed through the cavern. With the music off, everything echoed, and I could tell he hadn't meant to be that loud. I glanced over at Egon and could see the confusion on his face.

"Both of you," Taylor clarified, softer this time.

We both walked over to the bar and sat down. I had a feeling I knew what this was about, and my stomach hurt; it was twisted in such a knot. For someone who said our relationship needed to be kept secret, Egon hadn't done a good job of hiding it. Showing up here, defending me, and helping with my work. He was practically telling everyone with his eyes.

"Things have changed," Taylor said, his face looking tired. "And it's time to get everything out in the open."

"Taylor..." I began. Taylor held up a hand to silence me and then looked at Egon.

"I know you two have feelings for each other," Taylor said flatly. "I also know that you want to keep it a secret. Though I must say you are doing a shitty job of that." I felt my cheeks flush, but didn't speak.

"The rules in here are simple: we don't speak of it outside the speakeasy. If someone talks about what they saw here, we all die. So, stop trying to pretend here. It's just insulting."

Egon simply nodded. Meanwhile, my head was a whirl of thoughts and emotions. Our secret was officially out, and we had a place we didn't have to hide. Sure, it was the speakeasy, but it was still a big deal.

"Next," Taylor said with a sigh. "Ginny has told me about your concerns." Taylor's gaze was back on me. "I'll admit, I still don't like the idea of the girls being here, but you both have a point. I can't live forever, and I have seen that the president can punish those he chooses for no reason. It would be best if they were able to take care of themselves."

I looked over at Ginny and could see the smile plastered on her face.

"Starting tomorrow, I will be bringing the girls with me. Meridith and Gladis will help with serving and will handle the closing duties. Patty is too young, but I can't leave her alone. We will set up a table behind the bar for her to play at and a cot in the storage room if she falls asleep."

I nodded in agreement. Taylor had put a lot of thought into this. With the girls helping, I may actually have some evening time to myself.

"You will work the first hour," Taylor continued, pulling my attention back to him. You will help them learn the ropes and get people settled in. After that, your shift will be over."

"I only work an hour?" I asked, confused.

Taylor nodded and looked at Ginny. "You and I have fallen into a bad habit," he explained. "We take one night off a year and work ourselves nonstop. Other people want and need help. So, we are both going to take time for ourselves. I plan to work the same way you do: an hour on, then off. Once they're settled, the girls will alternate days so they don't work every day, and I've hired Tony to manage the bar. I'll still take a few full shifts here and there to give him a night off."

"You are trusting other people to run this place?" I asked, surprised.

"I'll still be here," he corrected. "Every night just in case, but if I'm not needed, I'll be enjoying what we've built and spending time with..." His voice trailed off, but I caught his eyes flick to Ginny for a fraction of a second. Ginny's cheeks flushed, and I couldn't help but smile. Was this really happening? Everything had already changed so much since the night before Assignment day. Now, I noticed myself feeling something I thought existed only in stories: happiness.

Chapter 19

"I must say," Felix said as he set his glass back down on the table, "this place is much nicer since the two of you stopped working all the time. More of a relaxed environment. Perhaps a place a person could do business."

"Don't even think about it," Taylor said as I sat down in my chair.

I had just finished my shift and was happy to join the others. Egon's arm immediately draped around my shoulders, and I felt all of the tension leave my body. It had been two weeks since Taylor held that late-night meeting, and things had fallen into an easy rhythm. The girls had taken to the jobs quickly, and both were finally excited to be helping. I had worried about how they would react to seeing Taylor with Ginny, but they all seemed just as taken with her as he was.

Egon had slowly allowed himself to relax. Inside the speakeasy, he was just a man and not the Captain. He stopped hesitating in showing affection and even seemed to have formed a friendship with Taylor. It was strange to hear him talking and even laughing so freely, but I loved it. Every night, he returned to my room with me and left before lights out. I found myself counting down the hours until the power cut off and I could be free to be with him and my real family once again.

Felix had become a regular member of our little group just a few days after the changes. He showed up, saying he had heard things were different and wanted to see for himself. Then he returned every night, joining us in drinks and laughs.

I relaxed in Egon's arms, watching my friends all enjoy themselves - the teasing, the smiles, and the laughs. It was a perfect moment. I didn't know it, but it would be the last one for quite a while. That's the thing about perfect moments: they are rare and tend not to last.

"There's been some tension of late," Felix's voice turned serious. "Talks about the rebels rising again."

"Rumors," Egon interjected. "We have found nothing to back that up."

I felt Egon's arm tense, the Captain returning to the surface. Damnit, Felix, way to ruin the mood.

"Still, you have to admit there's been a lot of strange and terrible things happening," Felix continued, not reading the room. "First, that tunnel collapse, then that *glitch* with the credit system, and now the President is in lockdown. Just saying, something is happening."

I shuddered to think of the tunnel collapse. Egon said that he would explain more once he figured out what happened. Yet, we had not spoken about it since. The glitch with the credit system had been chaos. Everyone's accounts were mysteriously credited with thousands of credits. When Egon tried to order the corrections made and the credits removed, the people started rioting. Instead, he decided to let the balances remain as a bonus. I knew he would find a way to make it up and get it back later. Still, people who needed the credits now benefited greatly. I had left mine in the account, prepared for the day the other shoe would drop, and I would need the cushion.

"It wasn't an accident," Egon said gruffly, fully back into Captain mode. "Blaylin ordered the collapse to thin out the *lesser* population. I confirmed it with a former guard who helped place the charges."

"Former?" I gaped at him.

"I eliminated a threat," Egon said flatly.

Everyone stared at their glasses in silence, the joy sucked out of the room.

"What about Blaylin?" I asked hesitantly.

Egon let out a heavy sigh. "Rumors are true. He has locked himself in the east wing of the manor. Only a few servants are allowed in, bringing us messages and orders from him."

"Even you aren't allowed in?" I gasped as Egon shook his head.

I could tell that everyone at the table felt just as uneasy about this revelation as I did. It was unheard of for Blaylin to do any business without his Captain at the ready.

Something big was happening, even if we had no idea what it could be. The tension in the air was palpable as everyone sat in silence.

"Has anyone ever told you you're a buzz kill?" I shot at Felix.

"My mother," Felix grinned. "But then again, she never did have a sense of humor."

Laughter broke out immediately. I felt Egon's arm relax as we all slid back into our comfortable and relaxed gathering. Meredith stopped by the table, refilling each of the glasses before hurrying off to another table. The conversation flowed effortlessly as everyone laughed. Around us, the speakeasy began to empty, and soon we were the only ones left.

"Time to close up," Taylor said as he stood up. "Finish up your drinks and clean up after yourselves."

"Finest services in the pit," Felix joked as he raised his glass.

Taylor moved toward the bar as the girls worked their way through the cavern, cleaning up. I felt Egon squeeze my shoulder, his signal that he was ready to head home for the night. I quickly finished my drink and prepared to stand and say good night when I caught movement by the storage room. The door was open, not cracked but fully open, and figures were moving inside. I glanced over and saw that Penny was sitting on the bar, telling Taylor something with a big smile on her face.

I looked back at the storage room just in time to see something being tossed out and the door slamming shut.

"GET DOWN!!" I yelled.

Taylor immediately grabbed Penny from the bar and ducked as everyone else dove to the floor. Egon grabbed my arm and pulled me downward, but it was too late. A bright light erupted in the cavern, followed by a wave of energy that hit me hard. I was knocked to the ground as pieces of debris and stone fell around me. My ears began ringing in a tone that felt like it was carving away at my brain. I tried to sit up, begging my eyes to see anything but white.

I had no clue what was happening, where Egon was, or whether everyone was all right. Just as I pushed myself up, a hand clasped over my mouth, and I felt myself being lifted off the ground. I fought back, trying to kick and claw my way out of the strange hands. I bit down on the one covering my mouth, the taste of copper immediately covering my tongue, but they did not let go. However, my bite broke through the glove, and the person's emotions flooded me. A sense of urgency, a hint of fear, determination, and pride.

Around me, I could hear people coughing, but my eyes still only saw white. I felt myself being carried away, powerless to stop it. I heard a metal door close, and then a cloth was wrapped around my eyes, plunging me into darkness.

Chapter 20

I felt her be ripped out of my grasp just as the white flash took away my sight. Blinded, I still tried to crawl in the direction she must have gone, desperate to find her. As I searched, I could hear footsteps around me, all staying just out of reach. Closing my eyes, I tried to access my gift, but all I could see was a white flash.

"Bridgett!" I yelled, causing myself to start coughing from the dust that was thick in the air.

I listened intently as the ringing in my ears began to lessen, and I could hear others moving around me. Slowly, my vision started to return. I rapidly blinked my eyes, willing it to come back faster. I straightened as I looked around the cavern. The tables and chairs were knocked over and pushed to the edges of the room. Judging by the black mark on the stone, that is where the explosion had come from.

My eyes quickly scanned the rest of the space. I spotted everyone, each still recovering from the explosion but unharmed, as they slowly began to gather—everyone except for her. Pushing myself up, I began to throw tables aside and look for her. Finally, my gift's access returned, and I searched the area, but she was nowhere to be found.

"Where is she?" Everyone froze as the words reverberated through the cavern.

I knew none of them had taken her, but there was no one else to direct my anger at. I watched each of them as they began sifting through the debris, not knowing that I knew she wasn't here without moving any of it—all of them except for one. Felix's eyes were as large as saucers as he stared at the supply room in the same direction Bridgett had been looking.

"Where is she?!" My voice reverberated off the walls as I closed the distance to Felix and grabbed him by the throat. His skin instantly turned white as he began clawing at my hand and gasping for air.

"Stop!" Ginny's shrill yell rang out. "We were all attacked!"

"He knows something." The words grinded out through my teeth that were pressed together so hard I was surprised they hadn't snapped.

"If he does, he can't tell you if he can't breathe!" Taylor yelled.

I wanted nothing more than to feel this prick's neck snap in my grasp. She had called him a friend, and he was involved in whatever the fuck just happened that took her away from me. Still, Taylor had a point. I let go of Felix and let him fall to the floor. He began coughing and holding his throat. I didn't move as I stared down at him. It was a good thing I didn't have my axe, or it would have already been in his skull. I had taken to leaving it in Bridget's room, trusting that it was safe there- a mistake I would not be making again.

"They were supposed to wait," Felix coughed as soon as he had taken a few deep breaths. "She's not ready."

Everyone else was silent, and I could hear the soft gasp that Ginny let out. I was right, the son of a bitch knew exactly who did this. That meant he knew where they took her.

"Where is she?" I growled as I leaned down closer.

"With the rebels," Felix quickly replied as he tried to move away from me.

I slammed my boot down on his hand to keep the worm in place. He let out a cry of pain and looked back at me. I could see the fear in his eyes. Good, he should be fucking scared right now. He had gotten comfortable with the version of me that sat here every night laughing and drinking with them. Little did he know that version only existed because of her. Without her, the monster was all that existed.

"You know where they are." I ground my boot into his hand, causing him to wince and cry out again as he shook his head.

"I only know they are on the surface," he cried. "They never shared how they travel in and out of the Underdark. All I get are messages and instructions."

I could tell the piece of shit was telling the truth. Still, that would not save him. I lifted my boot only to slam it down on his hand once more. He would pay for his part in this, but for now, I needed to find her. I walked across the cavern to the supply room. Nothing looked out of place. The walls were solid, and there was no way I could see for these rebels to get in and out.

"What do you mean she wasn't ready?" It was Taylor demanding answers when I walked back into the cavern. "You knew they were coming for her. She trusted you!"

Felix was holding his hand close to his body. I could see that the fingers were bent at incorrect angles; they were already swelling and bruising. It was broken. He could suffer with that pain while I found her, and then I would end him.

"They were always coming for her!" Felix shot back. "My job was just to make sure she was ready. I was to report back when she was ready to join the rebellion."

"Your job?" Ginny said, anger rising as she stepped forward. "Those files you requested. You used them to manipulate her, didn't you?"

"Not how you think," Felix choked out.

The sound of the slap echoed in the chamber. I hadn't even seen Ginny move, but it was obvious that she had smacked him. I felt a slight satisfaction in the look of hurt on Felix's face. It wasn't nearly enough, but it was a start.

"They were supposed to wait until I said she was ready to accept her place," Felix pleaded. "I kept reporting back that she wasn't and offering up others that were better suited to join their cause. They always rejected them and said they would wait for her."

"Apparently, they got tired of waiting," I said, causing all of the blood to leave his face once more.

"It would seem so," Felix nodded slowly.

"It still doesn't make sense," Taylor said as he held his daughters close. "She wouldn't have gone with them willingly. That girl would have fought them, and yet they got her out of here without leaving any indication they were even here."

Taylor was a genius. In my panic, I had only looked for enough blood to be a person. Taylor was right. My girl would have drawn blood on the bastards at the very least. Accessing my gift, I surveyed the stone floor. At first, all I saw was the expected old blood from past fights. Then I saw it, fresh drops glowing brightly. I followed the trail all the way to the supply room, where they suddenly stopped in the center of the room.

Bending down, I searched the stone floor. Through the dust, I noticed a slight gap. Breaking a board off a nearby crate, I shoved it into the gap and pried up the piece of stone. Underneath was a metal hatch. I pulled it open, the sound of scraping metal echoing around me, and peered down into the cavern below, where the blood trail continued.

"That's my girl," I breathed. "Keep giving them hell. I'm coming."

"What the fuck?!" Taylor gasped behind me.

I stood, not bothering to brush the dirt from my pants as I shut the hatch. "I need you to stand guard," I said as I pushed past him. "I'll go fetch my pickaxe and go after her. In the meantime, no one but me or her goes in or out."

I could tell he wanted to ask me how I found it, but decided against it. Instead, he looked over to where Felix was still sitting on the floor, Ginny standing over him like an angry bear.

"What about him?"

I looked over at the man shaking on the floor as he clutched his broken hand.

"Tie him up," I said as I looked away. "If I don't make it back, slit his fucking throat."

"And if you do?"

"He can answer to her."

I heard them moving Felix to a chair and tying him up. I made my way through the tunnels and into her room. It felt different without her here. Grabbing my pickaxe from where it sat beside the shelf, I saw one of the books sitting on the table.

She had finished Dracula a few days ago and had started on something else that I hadn't bothered to pay attention to.

As I turned to leave, the emptiness crushed down on me. I would get her back. She would get to finish those books and tell me all about them.

Chapter 21

"She better be worth all this trouble!"

I slammed into the ground as the men who were carrying me let me go. I had squirmed and kicked the entire time, and my body was exhausted. They had gagged me after I had bitten another one of them and drawn blood yet again.

"You know she's the only one who can open it!" the other shot back. "Now, go and fetch Nyla. She said they had to meet in the tunnel."

I heard the first man grumble and the sound of his footsteps as he left. From what I could guess, there was just the one now. I heard him remove the gag, and I was grateful to have whatever it was out of my mouth.

"You need to let me go," I said in my most pathetic-sounding voice. "If you don't, bad things are going to happen."

The man laughed, and I could feel that he moved closer. "Or what? You going to bite us again?"

"You wish," I said, shaking my head. "I'm sure it would be more enjoyable than what's coming for you."

The man let out a deep belly laugh as he stood back up and pulled off my blindfold. The light instantly hurt my eyes, and I had to slam them shut, wincing away from it.

"You idiot!" a woman's voice yelled. "She has never been above ground. She needed to be exposed slowly or risk losing her eyesight!"

The man's voice shook as I heard him take a few steps. "My apologies, ma'am," he stuttered. "I was only trying to make her comfortable and show her she was safe. That no one could follow her here."

The silence in the air was heavy. I wanted desperately to open my eyes and see what was going on, but kept them shut. I didn't fear the pain, but the thought of losing my sight kept my eyes closed. "Get out of sight!" the woman ordered. I heard the men leave hastily, and someone moved closer. A gentle hand gripped my shoulder. "You need to turn," the woman said softly. I pushed my body around and allowed her to guide me. When she squeezed my shoulder, I stopped. "Alright," she said. "You can open your eyes now. It will still be a bit too bright, but you will adjust since it's not direct."

"What's not direct?" I kept my eyes shut as the question burst out of me. I had never heard of lights that could burn someone's eyes or make them go blind. "The sun," the woman said softly.

Slowly, I opened my eyes, the light still a bit too harsh but bearable. I was looking at a stone wall of the tunnel, my shadow in front of me as the light filtered in from behind.

"The sun?" I asked slowly. "You brought me to the surface?"

The woman stood and wiped her hands on her pants. "You should have come here years ago," she answered.

"Your mother left clear instructions, but things got complicated. I do apologize that we couldn't wait for you to be ready, to ask you to come of your own free will. But things are getting more dire by the day."

I sat staring at my shadow as the woman explained. Her name was Nyla, and she was the rebels' commander. She said that everything I had been told about the surface was a lie. It was safe, and the radiation levels had been in a safe range for years. President Blaylin only kept up the pretense of danger to keep people from leaving the Underdark. He did assign a group of people to work the surface every year. Usually, troublemakers or those of no use to him were killed and disposed of immediately after leaving. Nyla and her people always tried to save as many as they could, but still, the soldiers were efficient in what they did.

None of that mattered to me, though. I was still hung up on something she had said. "My mother," I said softly. "You said she left instructions for me to be brought here."

Nyla sat down beside me and handed me a large metal box. "She said to give you this, and it would answer all your questions."

"What's inside?" I asked, taking the box from her.

"I have no idea," she admitted. "All we know is that it holds information that only you can access. Part of it is the information we need to bring down Blaylin and end the Underdark finally."

Carefully, I looked at the box. I saw no hinges or way to open it. I opened my mouth to ask Nyla how to open it, but when I looked over, she was gone. I turned my attention back to the box. Nyla wanted it open to get the information to bring down Blaylin. Before, I would have wanted the same thing. But hearing that my mother had left it for me, I wanted to see the message she had left. What was her explanation for leaving me in the tunnel and allowing me to be raised by Blaylin? How could she justify abandoning me to such a cruel fate?

I sat with the box for what felt like hours and was still no closer to opening it. Nyla reappeared, handing me a mug of clear, cool water that I drank.

"I can't open it," I said, trying to hand her the box back.

Nyla shook her head and put her hands in her pockets. "You will," she assured me. "You're the only one who can. Now, please follow me. Keep your eyes low and do not look directly up. It will take your eyes a few days to adjust."

"Where are we going?" I asked as I stood up, gripping the box.

"We have prepared a house for you," she said, stepping towards the mouth of the cavern. "I will take you there to get cleaned up and settled in."

"Settled in?" I gasped. "I can't stay here!"

"You have no choice," Nyla said as she looked at me sternly. "This is your home now."

Home. No, she was wrong. Home was where I fell asleep each night in Egon's arms. Egon! He would have found the blood trail, and I had no doubt he would come for me. He would kill the men who took me and then Nyla for ordering them

to, not to mention anyone else who tried to stop him.

"You need to let me go," I said firmly as I stood, leaving the box on the ground. "If you don't, he will kill you all."

Nyla let out a light laugh. "I don't know who you think is coming for you. No one in the Underdark can find our tunnels, and even if they did, it is a maze of death if you don't know the way. You are safe."

Well, at least I could agree with her on something; I was safe. Not because they thought they had me hidden away, but because I was the only person here that Egon wouldn't kill when he arrived. In perfect timing, a deep, guttural yell echoed through the cavern. It sounded like a crazed animal heading through the tunnels. He was still a ways away but was getting closer. "Bridgett!" His voice echoed around us. My heart leapt in my chest, and I could see the fear creeping across Nyla's face.

"You didn't account for him," I said flatly as I looked into the dark tunnels.

"No," Nyla said with a slight tremor in her voice. "That's not possible. No person has ever..."

"That's where you made a mistake," I retorted. "The second you took me from him, he stopped being a person. Now, the Captain, the monster, is hunting for me and will kill those responsible for taking me without mercy. If you let me go now, I will convince him to leave you all alone."

Nyla snapped her fingers, and several men filed into the cavern. "Take her to her lodgings," she ordered. "And collapse the tunnels."

Now it was my turn to be scared. If she sealed the tunnels, Egon wouldn't be able to reach me. I began fighting against the men who pulled me out of the cavern. Nyla picked up the box from where I had left it and followed us out. As soon as we were clear, explosions sounded from inside, kicking up a wave of dust that was impossible to see through.

Once it settled, I saw that the entrance to the cavern was gone. I felt a tear roll down my cheek, but only one. The rest instantly dried up from the anger that raged inside me. I fought harder against the men, like a wild animal caught in a trap. "Calm down," Nyla said in an even tone that sounded almost as if she were bored. "How about a deal? You open the box, provide the information we need, and we will reopen the tunnel so you can return to your monster. Sound good?"

Something in my gut told me that it was too easy. That collapse would take months to dig out. Still, fighting against them served no purpose. The blood would lead Egon to me. Even if he couldn't get through the way I had, I did not doubt that he would find another way. In the meantime, I was the one thing I hated most, helpless. I had no idea how to survive on the surface. I needed time for my eyes to adjust and to learn the basics. If I pretended to go long with the plan, I would be ready by the time Egon arrived.

Chapter 22

"My patience with you is growing thin," Nyla snarled. "Everyone here earns their keep. It's time for you to earn yours."

I threw the box, and it crashed to the floor. Whoever had made it had done an amazing job. The wood didn't splinter. According to Nyla, it was unbreakable. I was sure they had tried everything before kidnapping me, but I was out of ideas.

"Well," I shrugged. "That didn't fucking work. Unless you have some other ideas, perhaps it would be best if I went home."

Nyla glared at me as she picked up the box and thrust it back at me. "You're not going anywhere," she growled before turning and slamming the door to my hut.

I breathed out a heavy sigh as I turned and set the box on a small table. Carefully, I looked over each side, feeling for any grooves in the wood that might be a secret mechanism. Despite being a pain in my ass, it was beautiful. The wood had a silky texture I had never felt before. Each seam met up perfectly, and it was stained a deep black. Several carvings on the lid depicted a night scene. There was a scatter of stars along the top; beneath them was what I assumed was the small town I was in now, with its little huts. Then there was a deep, strong line separating it from a second picture. There were carved tunnels and layers that seemed to run deep underground, with flames at their bottom. It didn't take a genius to know that it was the Underdark.

Despite its beauty, I couldn't figure out how to open it. Part of me believed it might not be opened. Perhaps, whatever was inside was supposed to stay there.

I let out a sigh as I slumped down in the chair. It didn't help matters that I knew nothing about the box, like who made it or why my mother had hidden such important information inside. I had tried to ask Nyla several times, but each time she brushed me off. She claimed that it wasn't important, and I was stalling. Sure, because staying locked in this hut was my idea of a vacation. Nyla claimed it was because of my eyes and that I wasn't a prisoner. I knew it was bullshit.

If I weren't a prisoner, she wouldn't have sealed the only way I had back to Egon. It had been two days since the collapse, and during the night, I could still hear him screaming. It sounded dangerous, like a wild animal ready to attack.

I pushed up from my chair and made my way over to the window. The shutters were closed for my protection. My hand was surprisingly steady as I gripped one side and slowly cracked it open. I stood to the side, careful to stay out of the light that poured inside as if it might burn me. After taking a deep breath, I took small, cautious steps towards it. My skin instantly warmed under the sun's rays. Having lived in the Underdark for so long, I had been feeling a chill since arriving on the surface.

Closing my eyes tightly, I brought my face into the light and let the warmth spread through me. I didn't open them;

instead, I listened to the sounds around me. I had traveled in the dark enough to determine what was around me without being able to see. However, the sounds outside made no sense. Boards were rattling, the voices were loud, as if they were trying to speak over each other, strange metal grinding and hissing sounds mixing throughout everything else.

I had to see. Slowly, I peeked open one eye, and instantly the sun turned my vision from black to white. My hand instinctively raised to shield myself, and I cursed under my breath. Perhaps Nyla wasn't lying about me staying inside for my sight. No, that couldn't be right. Slowly, I blinked, keeping my hand up to protect myself from the harshest rays. With each blink, the blinding white disappeared, and the world began to fill in around me.

My breath caught in my throat as I leaned closer to the window, my hand still shielding me. It was like I had fallen asleep and slipped into a dream. There were more huts than I could count spread throughout, and from the sounds of it, more that I couldn't see. People walked in the streets, not in jumpsuits but in normal clothes. While their clothes looked worn, it was still a beautiful sight—no ugly jumpsuits worn to show your station. Children ran through the streets, playing games that had them laughing harder than I had ever heard a child laugh. The adults were busy doing various tasks. Some were chopping trees, while others banged against metal, worked on roofs, and performed other tasks I had no idea how to describe.

I leaned further, my face nearly outside the window. I was desperate to see more.

"Get back inside!"

I jumped, slamming the shutters closed. Of course, Nyla didn't trust me enough to go far. She stormed in the door a moment later, anger rolling off her in waves.

"Just what the hell do you think you're doing?!" she demanded as she slammed the door closed.

The surprise of her shrill voice had disappeared. I held my head high as I straightened up. "My eyes are adjusting just fine," I said matter-of-factly. "I wanted to see something outside of this hut."

"You will see what I say you can see."

She took a step forward, her chest rising and falling quickly with angry breaths. Her glare intensified as I stood my ground and didn't back away. "I can't open it," I said firmly. "And sitting here staring at it isn't going to change that."

Nyla didn't speak, and her posture only showed her anger rising. I could hear her teeth grinding as she took another step forward. She was now close enough that I could feel the heat of her breath on my face. She was slightly taller than I and was growing more frustrated that her intimidation wasn't working. She had no idea that I had seen worse, and her scare tactics were average at best.

"Listen here, you little shit!" I felt the mist of her spit as she leaned down closer to my face. My fist balled at my side, ready to make her move back if I had to.

BANG, BANG, BANG.

"Visitors!" someone called from the other side of the door.

Nyla glanced at the door and then back at me. "You will stay here and open it," she commanded. "You have two days. After that, we will detonate charges in the tunnels. Your boyfriend will die!"

"You bitch!" I lunged forward, letting my anger fuel my attack. Nyla was ready, side-stepping and shoving me to the ground. I rolled onto my back as I landed. As I went to push myself up, I let out a grunt as Nylan's foot landed on my chest.

"Two days," she repeated. She raised her foot and slammed it down once again.

I gasped for air as pain rippled through my chest. Nyla stepped back, smoothing her shirt and hair. I watched as she slid back on the mask I had seen when I first arrived. I didn't know who was here, but she obviously didn't want to show them her true self, yet. No, she would play the part of a gentle and understanding friend just as she had done with me. Then, the second they couldn't deliver what she wanted, they would see her for who she truly was. Her rot was just as deep and disgusting as Blaylins. At least he was upfront with his wickedness. Nyla was worse. The perfect actress, hiding the monster she truly was.

Chapter 23

One day left. One day had already passed of my deadline. I collapsed on the cot, my legs and feet exhausted and sore from stomping on the damned box. Nyla hadn't returned, probably too busy entertaining her guests. Not that she needed to. The terms were clear: open the box or Egon would die.

"Something doesn't sit right," a female voice faded in from outside my window.

"You're being paranoid," a deep male voice responded in a comforting tone. "This is no different than Twain."

I stood up from the cot and made my way closer to the window. I didn't dare to open the shutters again. Instead, I leaned my ear against the window and strained to listen.

"No," the woman said, her voice full of worry. "I can feel it. These are people together against a common enemy. Their fear is enough to make me sick. I have tried to calm them, but there is just too much."

"Alright," the man responded. "I trust you. What do we do next?"

The woman shushed the man, and I heard footsteps moving closer. I darted away from the window and scooped up the box from where it lay on the floor just as the door burst open. I looked up wide-eyed at a woman with fiery red hair and a look in her eyes that told me she had seen more than most people.

"Maddie!" a large man hissed as he ducked inside the door and grabbed her arm. "You can't just barge into people's homes!"

Saying the man was large was an understatement. The small hut suddenly felt too small as his head grazed the roof, and his broad shoulders, as if flexed, brushed the walls on either side.

"This isn't my home," I said without thinking.

The man looked at me in surprise. The woman, Maddie as he called her, didn't appear phased. She took a step forward, her eyes looking at me in a way that made me a little uneasy.

"You're not afraid," she finally spoke. "Everyone else here is afraid but you. You're pissed off."

I slammed the box down and stared at it for a moment. "Wouldn't you be pissed if you were kidnapped from your home and forced to open a box that can't be opened because your dead mother said you were the only one who could?" My breaths were coming heavy now as, for the first time, I let myself truly feel everything that had occurred over the past few days. "Oh, and if I fail to get it open, that crazy bitch is going to blow charges in the tunnels and kill the only person in this world who sees me, who loves me."

I felt the tears running down my face, but I didn't wipe them away. They weren't anything to be ashamed of, and I wore them with pride. They weren't tears of hate or sorrow but of love and longing.

"Tell us everything," Maddie said gently as she placed a hand on my arm. "We want to help."

I felt my emotions calm down, the boiling anger turning to a soft simmer instantly. Once my mind settled, I could sense her sincerity. I told them everything about living in the Underdark, Blaylin, and the speakeasy. I spoke of Egon and the others who had been there when I was taken, everything.

"Where is he?" the man asked, his voice steady but firm.

"Garrett," Maddie said hesitantly. "We need to be smart about this."

"Says the woman who ten minutes ago kicked in a stranger's door," he replied flatly while his eyes remained locked on me. "Where is he?"

I glanced at Maddie, who gave me a reassuring nod. "To the left," I said as I pointed at the door. "There's a cave opening not far from here. Nyla had the tunnel entrance collapse."

Garrett said nothing as he turned and left.

"Shit," Maddie said, shaking her head, "Here we go."

She sounded as if she was disappointed or upset, but I caught the small smile tugging on her lips. I followed her out the door. Garrett was walking with a mission as he walked straight to the cave. Maddie and I were jogging, trying to keep up with him.

"Garrett!" Nyla's voice rang out full of false joy. "I was hoping you and your lovely wife could join us for..."

Her voice trailed off as Garrett strode past her, not acknowledging her words. Nyla's eyes found Maddie next. Her look of confusion disappeared as she spotted me beside her.

"What have you done?" Nyla was trying to hide the venom in her voice, but she was failing. "Maddison, this girl is a new arrival. The poor thing is confused and brainwashed. What story did she make up this time?"

"We will know if it's true soon enough," Maddie said as she gently took my arm and led me past Nyla. "What is your name?" Maddie asked as we neared the cave entrance. Just ahead of us, Garrett had disappeared into the darkness.

"Bridgett," I answered, hoping she couldn't hear the shake in my voice. "Bridgett Coal."

A large grin spread over her face. "You're the one we came to see."

"You came to see..." My words cut off as a thunderous crash echoed inside the cavern. I felt the ground shudder slightly, and then it happened again.

"What is happening?" I gasped as Maddie pulled me back a few steps.

"Garrett," Maddie said with a look of pride. "That husband of mine can't stand for someone to keep couples apart. And by the sounds of it, you and Egon will be reunited shortly."

Another thunderous bang and the ground quivered. "How?" The question sounded as if it had been asked by someone else, lingering in the air.

"We're MUTS," Maddie explained, "Just like you. Garrett has never met a wall that he couldn't punch or kick his way through. Especially when he's pissed off."

Chapter 24

I felt myself jump a little as the thunderous bangs echoed through the earth. I tried to warn Maddie that he could cause another collapse. I could see the look of concern on her face, but she just shook her head.

"Nothing will stop him now," she said, looking back at the cave. "He's stubborn like that."

I followed her gaze just as the ground shuddered once more. Nyla was standing a short distance away, a look of hate in her eyes as she spoke to the men who had joined her. She was a problem for later. Right then, I had to stop Garrett. While I wanted nothing more than the mines to be opened back up, I wasn't willing to risk his life for it. He had literally just met me minutes ago.

I took off running towards the cave. I could hear Maddie yelling behind me, but I didn't look back. Garrett may be stubborn, but so was I. I knew I should have been cautious instead of running into a cave with a man who could literally punch his way through stone. However, in that moment, caution was not in my vocabulary.

The cave shook hard as I ran inside, and small rocks and dirt fell from the ceiling. I straightened my eyes until I spotted him. Garret was pulling his fist away from the wall. He was already several feet into the tunnel. I ran closer and reached him just as he pulled back and struck the wall again. I watched as it turned to rubble and a few more feet opened up.

"Stop!" I yelled while trying not to cough on the debris.

"Go back outside with Maddie," Garrett ordered as he shook his hand. Even in the dim light, I could see the blood that covered his fist splashed onto the walls.

"You're going to kill yourself!" I argued. "If not from a collapse, then bleeding to death!"

Garrett looked back at me. I could still see the rage in his eyes, but it had softened. "It's just a few more feet," he said slowly. "Just a few more hits and it will be open."

"Or the whole thing could come crashing down!"

Garrett took a step towards me, pressing his bleeding hand against his pants. If blood loss didn't kill him, surely infection would. I reached for his hand, but he drew it back. I looked up at him and couldn't understand the expression on his face.

"I hope you'll forgive me."

Before I could ask what for, I felt his large hands grab me around the waist and toss me. It wasn't a hard throw, and I landed on the ground near the cave entrance. I rolled through the landing, unharmed. I could see Maddie arguing with Nyla, her fiery red hair moving around chaotically as she spoke. I looked back at the cave and pushed myself up.

"Seize her!" Nyla's voice rang out.

There was no time. I took off running back into the cave just as the ground shuddered again. This time, it felt deeper. Almost as if the vibration rattled all the way through the earth. I wouldn't be surprised if that one were felt in the Underdark. Larger pieces of rock fell from the ceiling around me. I glanced up just in time to see one directly above me fall. There wasn't time to run, and it looked larger than me. Ducking down, I put my arms over my head and braced for the hit.

The sound of shattering stone filled the air just as another body covered mine. I leaned into Garrett as he shielded my body with his, hitting away what he could and taking the impact of what he couldn't. It felt like hours we were trapped like that when it was probably only seconds. When the earth finally stilled and the rocks stopped falling, I dared to open my eyes.

The air was still thick with dirt and dust. Despite that, I could see a familiar figure standing at the tunnel entrance.

"Egon," I breathed, allowing tears to run down my face.

Garrett turned to look, his body still shielding mine. Egon moved faster, slamming into Garrett and knocking him to the ground.

"Egon!" I yelled as I pushed myself up and ran over to where he had Garrett pinned to the ground. I knew Garrett could have flung Egon off of him like an annoying bug. Instead, Garrett raised his arms and protected himself from the most vicious blows. "Egon, stop! He helped me! He was protecting me!"

Egon's fist froze midswing as he looked back at me. In his eyes, I could see it, the Captain. I walked closer and placed my hand on his shoulder. His body remained tense, but he allowed me to lead him away from Garrett.

"What the fuck?!" Maddie's voice echoed as she joined us.

I didn't look back. I kept my gaze focused on Egon as I put more distance between him and Garrett. I saw Maddie rush to Garrett out of the corner of my eye. She looked furious but said nothing else.

"He took you," Egon growled as he looked back at Garrett.

"No," I said firmly, grasping his hand.

"It wasn't him. He and his wife were helping me get back to you."

Egon didn't relax, but as he looked back at Garrett, I could see the hint of apology in his eyes.

"It's all good," Garrett laughed as he stood up, blood still dripping from his hand. "Can't say I would have reacted any differently if it were Maddie."

Egon looked back at me, and I could see his eyes roaming over me. "I'm fine," I insisted. "They didn't hurt me."

I took a step forward, desperate to be in his arms. Egon took a step back, holding me away from him. I wanted to yell at him, demand comfort, but then I felt it. His emotions thrust into me as if he were forcing me to feel them. His rage was like nothing I had ever felt before. I could feel what he wanted to do to those who took me. I could also feel he yearned to hold me as much as I yearned to be held. But if he let himself do that, it would cool off some of his rage. He needed it to do what he felt had to be done.

I had only seen this side of him once before, outside the speakeasy with Shawn. For the first time, I noticed the pickaxe that was in his hand. I was relieved that he hadn't used it on Garrett. However, I suspected it was because he wanted Garrett to feel pain before he killed him. Is that what his plan was-to beat the persons responsible until they were close to death and then kill them with his pickaxe? I felt myself shudder at the thought. Nyla was a bitch, but I wasn't sure she deserved that. Without thinking, I allowed my eyes to move to where she was standing just outside the cave.

"Stay here," Egon ordered as he pushed me behind him and began to take large strides towards Nyla. I watched, frozen where I stood, as he approached her without a word and grabbed her by the throat. The men around her moved to help, but all fell instantly to their knees. I could see the blood running out of the corners of their eyes as they cried out in pain.

"What the fuck?!" Maddie gasped as she took in the sight.

"Egon and I are MUTS," I explained. I still had no idea what the word really meant, but I wanted to make sure Maddie and Garrett understood. "And he's pissed."

"Ya think?" Garrett gasped. "We need to stop him."

"Why?"

The question and the casual way it came out of my mouth surprised me.

"Something is going on here," Maddie said in a rushed voice. "Without her, we have no chance of figuring it out."

"Once we know what's going on, he can do whatever he wants with her for all we care."

Something deep inside me knew they were right. As I looked back at Egon, I could see that Nyla and the others didn't have much time left. I ran towards him, gripping his arm firmly as I tried to pull it down. Egon didn't look at me, and I wasn't sure if he even knew I was there.

"Stop!" I begged. "Not yet! We need her!"

Egon's gaze turned to me, and I felt a shiver run down my spine. He was angry, this time with me for asking him to stop.

"Please," I begged, tugging on his arm once more.

With a huff, he let go of Nyla. She fell to the ground hard and immediately began gasping for air. The guards' screams turned to whimpers as their blood stopped spilling from their eyes.

"Not yet," Egon said as he pulled me closer to him. I nodded in understanding.

He was letting them live for now because I asked. But he would have his vengeance, and I just agreed not to stop him.

Chapter 25

The air was silent as we headed into town. Everyone was outside, probably alerted by the tremors that Garrett had caused. They all watched us as we walked through town with Nyla and her men. The men still had blood staining their faces. Nyla was still gasping for air, a stark hand print around her throat. No one asked questions or tried to stop us as we made our way to the center of town. Instead, they all followed behind, surrounding us in a tight circle when we stopped.

"They're terrified," Maddie whispered as she looked back at the gathered crowd. "And not because we have their leader. In fact, they are less scared than they were earlier."

I looked back at the people and saw fear in their eyes. I thought this was a place where rebels had come together to fight against the Underdark, against Baylin. If that were the case, shouldn't they be upset that their leader was gasping for breath? Why would they be less afraid?

Questions swirled in my mind as I looked back at Maddie. In that moment, there was only one question that I needed the answer to.

"You said you were looking for me. Why?"

Maddie's eyes locked with mine, and her expression softened. "That's a bit of a long story," she said softly. "And some of the pieces are still missing." I followed her gaze as she looked back at where Nyla was sitting. "However, I think I know who has them."

I followed Maddie as she walked closer to Nyla, Garrett, and Egon, close at our sides. Nyla was rubbing her throat as she looked up at us with hatred.

"Did you know the girl you claimed to have never heard of was here the whole time?" Maddie asked in a condescending tone. "You had to have, considering you kidnapped her and were holding her hostage."

"Fuck you," Nyla spat.

Maddie looked unfazed as she kneeled on Nyla's level, staring into her eyes. The silence around us was heavy as neither of them said a word. I was just about to speak when Maddie stood up.

"Here's what I'm able to get," she began, never looking away from Nyla. "You loved someone but weren't able to give him what he needed. So, he found someone who could, and that made you jealous. This jealousy led you to murder someone, which a small part of you regrets, to take over as leader of the rebellion. However, the people did not answer you as they did the others, and that pissed you off. Not as much as not being able to get what you needed to win back your love. So, you ruled over this town with fear until you were able to get what you needed. You were so close, too."

Nyla's eyes grew wide as Maddie spoke. The specific details were missing, but the general overview was enough to make Nyla nervous. Angry rumbles rose from the gathered crowd, and Nyla looked around in panic.

"Who?" I demanded, leaving my question deliberately vague.

Nyla glanced back at me and then the crowd. "They'll kill me," she hissed. Egon moved fast, swinging his pickaxe down into one of Nyla's men's skulls. The man went limp instantly and crumpled lifeless to the ground. Egon pulled out his weapon and stepped back to stand beside me. I looked back at Nyla and could see she was visibly shaken.

"Clarissa," she said just above a whisper. "And your father."

Clarissa, my mother. Nyla had killed my mother to become the leader of the town. Did that mean my mother was the leader of the rebellion? I wanted to ask, but another question blurted out. "Who's my father?"

Nyla looked uncomfortable. I was in no mood for stalling. Maddie had said that

Nyla was trying to win him back. That meant he was still alive.

"Who is he?!" I yelled, grabbing her by the front of the shirt.

I saw her lips move, but her voice was too light to hear. I leaned closer, and she whispered it once more. "Blaylin."

My blood turned to ice in my veins. Letting her go, I took a step back. Egon was there instantly, wrapping his arm around me to steady me. I stared at her in disbelief. It couldn't be true. That vile man could not be my father. I was an orphan, and he had spent my whole life torturing me.

"He needed an heir," Egon said softly. "A male heir. If he only had a daughter, it makes sense what his plan was. Forcing us together to make him a male heir. It would be blood related to him, and then he would not need us."

My body began to shake as my rage simmered. I hated that bastard before, but somehow it was worse now.

"What's in the box?" I demanded.

Nyla began laughing as if she had gone insane. "Everything your mother fought so hard for. The documents for the breeding program, the codes to access the secret database, and who knows what else. That bitch had everything Blaylin needed to secure his position and eliminate the rebel threat!"

"You were going to hand it and all these people over to him," Garrett spoke up. "All in hopes that he would want you?"

"I'll give him a son!" Nyla yelled. "A true heir. A strong heir. I need to prove to him that I can be trusted."

I couldn't listen to any more. I turned and stormed back to my hut. Once a prison, it now served as a shield. I heard Egon walk in behind me, but I paid him no attention. I walked over to where the box was and picked it up. Nothing about it had changed. I wasn't sure whether I wanted to know what was inside it. Nyla said the rebels had secrets that could harm Blaylin. But my mother was also the woman who lay with that piece of shit and conceived me. How could I trust anything she had done or left me in this box?

"Nyla mentioned a breeding program," Egon spoke behind me. I turned to face him, tears burning in my eyes. "She may not have been a willing participant."

I looked away from him and back at the box. He had a way of reading my mind tonight that was a bit unnerving. Still, he wasn't wrong.

Looking at the box, I found myself staring at the carving once more. There was the town and the Underdark. In the center was a raindrop shape. I had thought it was the key to unlocking. However, placing water on it did nothing. Perhaps it didn't mean water.

"I need my blood," I said, holding my hand out to Egon. He looked at my hand and back at me, not moving. "I think the key to unlocking this thing is in my blood. Blood of someone from above and below."

Egon stepped closer and looked at the carving. After a few minutes, he nodded in agreement. Gently, he took my hand and pressed the tip of my finger to his pickaxe. It was just enough to bring a drop of blood to the surface. After taking a deep breath, I pressed my bloody finger to the symbol. Something clicked inside the box, and the lid separated.

"It worked," I gasped.

I set the box on the table and looked at it as if it might explode. I had it open, and now I had to decide what to do with what was inside. If I read it, there was no going back. My hands shook as I slowly opened the lid and looked inside. I could see a couple of leather-bound books, their pages brittle. But on top was a folded letter with *BRIDGETT* written on it. I lifted it out and sat on my cot. I felt the cot dip as Egon joined me, placing a protective arm around me. After taking a deep breath, I unfolded the paper.

Chapter 26

The script inside was elegant, full of smooth loops and tight curls. My mother would have been ashamed if she saw the chicken scratch that was my handwriting. I forced myself to focus and began to read.

My Dearest Bridgett,

As I write this, I know that I will never be able to look upon your face again. I know by the time this finds you, your life will have been unbearable. I'm not sure what your father will have told you about me, if anything. There is a chance nothing I can say will change your mind, but I have to try. I have to believe that my spark lives on in you.

My name is Clarissa Coal. I was raised on Level One of the Underdark. My parents, Marvin and Theresa Coal, were good people. They gave me the best education and all the love a child could ever dream of having. My father was a councilman, a legacy to one of the founders. He was considered an outcast by his peers, refusing to implement anything that ran counter to the original doctrine that founded the Underdark. He and my mother stood for the values the city was built on, and in the end, it cost them their lives.

Blaylin learned after years of trying that he was unable to have children naturally. Doctors were able to perform a procedure that would give him a ten percent chance of producing a child. However, the materials wouldn't last long enough for his mistress to be the only one who tried. On a tight schedule, it was suggested that he choose ten potential mothers of good health and standing to be inseminated. Many other young women begged for a chance to be one of his chosen ones, but I was not one of them.

I saw the opportunity for what it was, a breeding program. Blaylin sought me out and demanded that I participate. My parents supported my decision, and my father fought to have the samples destroyed as their use in this manner was unethical. I believe that this was what led to their deaths. I found them both, killed in our home, just a few days later. Blaylin came for me immediately. I don't remember much of what happened. I was strapped to a table while doctors performed the insemination.

    Afterward, Blaylin insisted that I be held with other potentials for my safety. I pleaded with him to allow me to put my parents to rest with a promise that after I returned, he would receive my full support and cooperation. His greed and ego overtook common sense, and he allowed me to. I didn't attend my parents' cremation; I ran. I hid in the tunnels of The Pit, begging for food and shelter. It wasn't long before my worst fears were confirmed; I was pregnant.

    I thought so many times about ending the pregnancy, convincing myself that the child was just another version of Blaylin. However, I could never bring myself to do it. As you grew, I could feel the love coming from inside me. I decided then that you weren't his child but mine. I would protect you from his cruelty and make this world a better place.

It was towards the end of my pregnancy that I first found the Speakeasy. The owner took pity on me and let me sleep in the supply room. It was in that room that you were born. I can still see your tiny face every time I close my eyes. I had so much love and hope for you that I forgot we were being hunted. You were only three days old when they came.

I was on my way back from the stalls, having just purchased you a blanket with your name on it. You were cooing softly as we walked. Everything was ordinary until it wasn't. Soldiers surrounded us, and I remember clutching you to my chest. I fought and screamed, but was overpowered. I felt my heart break that day as they pulled you out of my arms.

The soldiers beat me badly and left me for dead. I barely made it back to the speakeasy. I begged the owner for help, and I could tell by the sorrow in his eyes that my fight was hopeless. I had lost you, and there was no way to get you back. I can still remember clearly as he took my hand and led me to the storage room. I watched as he lifted a plate from the floor, revealing a tunnel. He told me to go to the surface. I couldn't give you a good childhood, but I could ensure your future. I had no idea what he meant, but I did as he said.

When I first came out of that cave, there were just a few run-down shacks and nothing else. In one of them, I found journals. I have included them in this box for you. It spoke of a planned rebellion, ways to contact other rebels, and the Underdark's weaknesses. The last rebels failed because they had too few numbers. Blaylin had just come to power, and people did not realize how bad things were. Blaylin had sent a group of soldiers to the surface and killed the few that lived here.

With this information and drive to give you a better future, I got to work. I fixed the huts and began building the rebel base needed. Outcasts were sent through the tunnel for years to join our cause. People like me, whom Blaylin had destroyed, were ready to fight back. I built everything with my best friend by my side. She had sought me out after I disappeared and eagerly joined the cause.

For years, I thought we were building something together. It wasn't until recently that I realized Nyla's true motive. She was Blaylin's mistress, and her fertilization had failed. She had been with him when you were brought in, and Blaylin dismissed her. He claimed he would wed only the mother of his child. She has been working ever since to bring us down. She believes that if she gives him the rebels and I am dead, he will give her what she wants.

There is a rumor that Blaylin may be able to produce one more sample, and she is desperate for it. If she can convince him to give it to her and produce an heir, she will get what she has always dreamed of. I am ashamed to say that I trusted and cared for this coward of a woman. Thankfully, I had the foresight to hold the secrets she needs close. After today, you will be the only one able to access them. I have used my gift, and the wooden lid of this box will only open to your blood.

I am sorry I am not there to explain all of this to you. The signs began to appear a few days ago, and I do not have much time left. The poison is working its way through my system, and there is no way to stop it. I fear that I will not see another dawn.

Please know, my dear daughter, that I love you and everything I have done has been for you. I am sorry I couldn't give you the better world you deserve. Instead, I leave you with the tools you will need to create that world for yourself. I have sent a coded message via a secure channel, declaring you the true leader of this rebellion. There are others out there, but they are not in a position to help as they are fighting their own battles. However, they have assured me that as soon as they are able, they will look for you.

I wish I could give you more, but I'm afraid my time has run out. The day of my parents' murder was the worst day of my life. I didn't want to live and being used as I was only made me more desperate to join them in death. You, my sweet girl, gave me not only the will to go on but a purpose. You are the center of everything, and I know you will go on to do amazing things.

I love you,

Clarrissa Coal

A tear slid down my face and landed on the paper. Clarrissa had been used and hurt by Blaylin just as much as I had. Reaching into the box, I pulled out the two thick, leather journals. I let a few more tears fall as I slid my hand over the covers, imagining my mother doing the same thing.

"It's time," I said, sliding the journals

back into the box. I closed the lid, wiping my blood from the mark, and heard the lock click back into place. "But I want to help kill the bitch."

Chapter 27

"I couldn't agree more," Maddie said as she walked into the hut, Garrett right behind her. "That woman makes my skin crawl. Her emotions are sickening to feel."

I snapped my head up and stared at her. I wasn't sure that I had heard her right.

"You can feel her emotions?" I asked. Without touching her?"

"I can," Maddie nodded. "Wait, can you feel emotions too?"

I nodded and looked at Egon. His arm was tight around me, ready to protect me if needed. We were raised that our gifts could be used against us if we talked about them. Yet, here I was telling Maddie openly about mine. She was easy to talk to. They had already seen part of Egon's gift, so it didn't seem like there was a need to hide mine.

"And you have to touch someone to

feel them?" Maddie continued as if this weren't a tense conversation. "And change them?"

"Just feel," I said softly. "You can change them?"

"I can," Maddie nodded. "But yours might work differently. You tend to get more control over your gift once you can project."

I laugh escaped my throat, but there was no joy in it. Blaylin had shown us how powerful a gift could be when you could project it. Knowing he was my father, I didn't want to. What if somehow his corruption was inside me as well? No, I would never let myself become like him.

"Not going to happen," Egon whispered to me.

That was it. "How are you doing that?" I demanded as I turned to look at him. "You seem to know what I'm thinking. It's been happening since you came out of the tunnel."

"You," he said as he cupped my cheek. "You have been pushing your emotions onto me since you stopped me from killing that man. I didn't know you could do that."

"Neither did I," I gasped, trying to figure out how I was doing it.

Maddie and Garrett watched us in silence as we spoke. I couldn't help but feel as if they understood what we were going through. Not because I could feel their emotions, but the look of understanding on their faces.

"I don't want to," I finally said. "Who knows what it could do? Who I could hurt?"

"Only one way to find out," Garrett offered. "You need to practice."

"You want me to practice on Egon, not knowing what could happen?"

"Of course not," Garrett said, holding up his hands in defense. "But we do have someone who deserves to suffer that would make a good test subject."

It took me a minute to register what he was saying. "You want me to practice projecting emotions on Nyla?" I asked slowly.

"Why not?" Maddie shrugged. "That woman could stand to feel a bit of emotion."

I sat, twisting my hands as I thought about what they were suggesting. I could tell from Egon's silence that he agreed with them. Otherwise, he would have told them to fuck off. Instead, he sat holding me and waited for me to make my own decision.

Slowly, I stood up, rubbing my hands on my pants. "I'll try," I finally agreed. Egon joined me, and together we followed Maddie and Garrett back to where Nyla still sat on the ground. Her hands were bound now, but the venom in her eyes had not diminished.

"Did you open it?" she spat as soon as she saw me.

I kneeled, looking at her as I allowed my emotions to surge through me. "You killed her," I said firmly. "You killed her and left me with that monster." I could feel the hate and anger radiating off me. I had no idea what I was doing, but nothing seemed to have changed. Nyla continued to glare back at me. I thought about the letter, all the pain Blaylin had caused, and the fact that Nyla had played a significant role in my suffering.

Nyla suddenly let out a scream that curdled my blood. I didn't react as I kept my gaze fixed on her, feeling all the pain and suffering I had endured over the years.

"Stop!" Nyla shrieked as she held her hands on her head. "Stop!"

"It hurts, doesn't it?" I said, not allowing my mind to wander. "I had years to learn to adapt, to take everything and become stronger. You, you're getting it all at once."

"You little bitch!" Nyla screamed. "Stop this!"

I didn't. I could feel my anger and hate slowly fading as I watched her feel the pain I had suffered through my entire life. My burden had barely been lifted when Nyla fell silent, and her body slumped to the ground. Her eyes were frozen open, and I could still see the suffering in their lifeless sheen. I stood just as the men around us began to scream. I glanced and could see the blood running down their faces. It didn't take long before their screams stopped, blood spilling across the ground at my feet.

Egon took my hand, and I could feel that his own anger had subsided—no need to burden him with the fact that mine was still simmering. We began to walk away, the blood squishing under our feet, when Maddie grabbed my arm.

"You need to talk to them," she said in a hushed tone.

I looked around at the rebels that were still standing gathered around us. The fear in their eyes was striking as they looked at the bodies and then at me.

"I can't," I said flatly.

"You have to," Maddie insisted. "They need you just as much as you need them. Your mother said you were the leader of this rebellion. If you don't do it, then it is over."

Egon squeezed my hand. "I don't want to lead," I replied. "You do it."

"I can't," Maddie said, shaking her head. "I'm not one of them, but you are. Garrett and I will help however we can, but you have to lead."

I looked back at the people, now staring at me, waiting for a sign that I would be the person they needed. Deep down, I knew I wasn't. I was the daughter of the man they were fighting against. But I was also the daughter of the woman who brought them all together.

"Lizzy and Cal didn't want to lead either," Garrett spoke up. "And they had been prepared their entire lives for it. But in the end, they did, and it was exactly what was needed to free our people."

I looked up at Egon. He wasn't saying anything. He was leaving this decision up to me, the bastard. I looked around at the people once more, my own confusion and insecurities swimming through my mind. I couldn't leave and go back to how things were. That left me with only one option.

"Let's get this trash cleared out of here," I said loudly, motioning towards the bodies. "We will gather here tomorrow at noon. This has gone on long enough. It is time for us to finish this. To bring our people out of the dark and drag the secrets into the light!"

A cheer erupted from the people, causing my heart to beat hard in my chest. I had no idea what I was going to do, but I knew I had to do something. I glanced at Egon, who nodded at me with a half-smile. He was ready to stand with me. That was all I needed to stand a little straighter as I looked out at the crowd. Blaylin had no idea what the little girl he tried to break was about to do to his perfect little world.

Chapter 28

Night came quickly, and the sounds of the town died down. I had spent most of the evening in my hut, reading through the journals my mother had left. She was right; the information they contained would play a major role in taking down Blaylin. According to the journals, several secret mine shafts led into the Underdark. They were originally meant as escape routes in the event of a catastrophic collapse. Their entrances were hidden years ago to keep them secure.

Blaylin clearly didn't know of their existence. If he did, they would have been destroyed and sealed years ago. At each location, there were notes in my mother's handwriting stating that she had checked that each was still usable.

"We won't use them all," Garrett said, pointing at the map. "Your numbers are too few to divide up that much. I suggest three points of attack."

I watched as he pointed at three of the entrances.

"Four," Egon said as he pointed at one more. I looked down and knew the tunnel he had chosen, one that I hadn't been able to stop thinking about. It came out in the president's cavern, Blaylin's home. "Bridgett and I will enter through this one, cutting the head off the snake."

"It should work," Maddie added thoughtfully. "His soldiers will be scattered to deal with the breaches. You shouldn't meet much resistance."

"Except for him," I breathed.

I had already filled Maddie and Garrett in on Blaylin's gift. There was a strong chance that he would crush us before we even got close. Our only hope was that our gifts together were enough to overpower him. I felt confident that Blaylin had never felt true emotion in his life, so there was a good chance it would confuse him. And, as far as we knew, he didn't know what Egon's gift was.

"We will go with you," Garrett nodded.
"We can't ask you to do that," I insisted.

"You didn't," Maddie smiled. "Besides, this isn't our first time fighting a corrupt government. We could use the excitement."

Garrett smiled as he pulled Maddie close and kissed the top of her head. I felt a surge of hope. When this was over, I wanted to be happy like they were. I wanted to be Egon's wife and be together until our final rest. However, I had no idea whether he was interested in a life like that. It was hard to imagine the Captain putting down his pickaxe, putting on a ring, and helping to change nappies.

"That's enough for tonight," Egon's voice growled. "We need some time alone."

Garrett nodded as he left with Maddie. I let out a sigh and looked down at the papers. I had allowed myself to get distracted by childish fantasies.

As soon as the door shut, Egon moved swiftly across the room. I hadn't realized how close he was until I found myself pinned between him and the wall of the hut. Instantly, I felt a heat surge in my core as his hand firmly gripped my throat.

"Projecting such things when we're not alone," Egon growled as he leaned closer to me. "I was able to control myself and ask them to leave."

Oh shit! I had done it again, projecting my feelings on him without realizing it. It took effort to project them onto Nyla, but with Egon, it happened without me even meaning to.

"You are the reason I will kill that son of bitch," Egon growled. "I will melt that fucking axe down to make our rings if that's what you wish. And I will give you children until you beg me to stop!"

My core clenched at his words. He wasn't angry that I wanted these things. He was angry that I was questioning whether he wanted to give them to me.

Since he had emerged from the tunnel, he had done as I asked, letting me take the lead and make the final decisions. It was time to let him take charge in the best way possible.

"I'm yours," I said softly, causing the heat in his eyes to flare.

"Mine," he growled back before crashing his mouth against mine.

Everything else melted away instantly. There wasn't an army of rebels outside—no war to fight in the morning. There was just him and his body pressed firmly against mine. He poured all his lust into the kiss, forcing my face up to deepen it. A moan escaped from his mouth as the ecstasy swirling inside me became too much to contain. He pressed harder against me, letting me feel that he was just as aroused.

He broke the kiss and turned towards the table in the center of the room. I eyed the cot and instantly realized it wouldn't hold both of us. Egon was already ahead of me. I turned my attention as everything that was on the table was swept to the floor in one fluid motion. He turned back to me, grabbing my hips and lifting me to sit on the table.

He wasted no time as he grabbed the hem of my shirt and pulled it over my head. I was desperate to remove his clothing as well, but managed to resist. He was in charge, not me. His eyes locked on mine as he undid my pants. I lifted myself slightly so he could slide them off, keeping my hands on the table. It was torture not touching him, but the look in his eyes told me he was testing me.

"Good girl," he rumbled after a few moments. "You ready for your prize?"

I nodded eagerly as he lifted his shirt, revealing his chiseled body. My mouth began to water as my gaze followed the lines of his muscles. My breath hitched as I realized that he had already removed his pants. It didn't matter how many times I saw him this way; it never got old.

"Lean back," he instructed as he pulled me closer to the edge of the table. I did as he said, propping myself on my forearms.

My heart was pounding in my chest as he dropped to his knees between my thighs. I watched as, with a wicked grin, he began to devour me. My head fell back as another moan escaped my lips. This only seemed to encourage him. His tongue moved more quickly in circles around my clit, bringing me closer to the edge.

I was ready for him to pull away, to deny as he had done before. However, the assault continued as he slid two fingers inside me. My fingernails dug deep into the table as my orgasm reached its peak and came crashing down. Egon slowed, working me through every delicious moment. When my body finally stopped clenching, he withdrew. I looked down at him, my legs trembling and my breathing heavy.

I watched as he stood and wrapped my legs around him. He positioned himself, locking his gaze with mine. My legs tightened around him as I watched him slide his fingers into his mouth, tasting my excitement as if it were a delicious meal.

He took his time, leaving me begging for him to be inside me. He smiled at me as he gripped my thighs and pulled me slightly forward and thrust into me.

The sudden fullness took away what little resolve I had left. I could feel myself already squeezing around him as he thrust in and out of me. One hand released my thigh and slowly traveled up my body to my neck. I leaned my head back as he gripped my throat once more—a death sentence for anyone else. But for me, it was his way of claiming me, showing me that he would never let me go.

"Say it," he breathed as his pace quickened.

"I'm yours," I gasped, feeling my orgasm reach its peak once more.

"And I'm yours," he replied with a greedy thrust. With that, my orgasm washed over me once more. Moments later, his movements became jerky, and I knew he had reached his as well. Still, he continued to move slowly inside me, ensuring that I enjoyed every moment.

If this is what the future holds for us, nights of doing this and being together, then morning couldn't come fast enough. I was ready to get this fight over with and stay with him forever.

Chapter 29

Sunrise came too soon. The cot in her hut was too small for both of us to sleep. I had tried to get her to lie in it, but she insisted on joining me on the floor. I could feel her bare skin on mine as her limbs wrapped around me. She had me constricted like she was afraid I might disappear during the night. I opened my eyes, ready to find a way to untangle myself and get my day started.

My eyes had barely parted when a bright white flash took over my vision. A burning spread throughout my head, radiating from my eyes that felt like fireballs inside my skull. I slammed my eyes shut, letting out a string of curse words. I hoped that closing them would suffocate the fire in my head. The pain eased, becoming an annoying sting.

"Turn towards the wall," Bridgett's voice said firmly.

I could feel her hands on my shoulders as she guided me. I kept my eyes pinned shut. The pain was nearly gone, but I wasn't risking it once again.

"It's alright," Bridgett assured me. "Your eyes just need time to adjust. You can open them now."

Slowly, I eased my eyes open. I was staring at the back wall of the hut, the light pouring in around me.

"Since when does light burn my damn eyes?" I spat. I wasn't angry with her, and I instantly regretted my tone. I was ashamed that I had been rendered useless and in need of saving from fucking light.

"It's the sun," she explained, her tone soft. I breathed a sigh of relief that I hadn't hurt her feelings. "It's quite a bit brighter than the lights we're used to. It won't take long to adjust. You have to take your time."

I huffed and crossed my arms. I hated being held back by something so trivial. I heard her giggle as she stood up and began getting dressed.

"I'll go fetch us something to eat," she smiled, bending down to kiss me. "Sitting here pouting isn't going to change that; you just have to be a little patient."

"I'm not pouting," I shot back.

"Then what would you call it?" She was still laughing at me as she stood up. I looked down, my knees drawn to my chest with my arms crossed. I was still naked from the night before, but thankfully, the sheet was draped over my lap, giving me some modesty. I let out a huff as I realized she was right. I looked like a child pouting, but I refused to say the words.

"That's what I thought," she smiled as she headed for the door. "Just don't let the light hit you directly in the face while I'm gone. Once we are done eating, we will be able to start working you closer to it."

I heard the door shut as she left. This was bullshit. She was out fetching food while I remained trapped, like a damsel hiding from the sun. If anyone found me like this, I would look directly at the sun and allow it to finish what it started.

Keeping my gaze down, I found my clothes where they lay on the floor. I pulled them and felt a bit more secure. At least if anyone came in, I wouldn't be naked.

It wasn't long after that when Bridgett reappeared. She motioned for me to sit at the table with my back to the window. I did as she asked, a slight smile tugging on my lips. I watched as she laid out fruits and bread for us before sitting down across from me.

"What are you smiling about?" she asked as she took a bite out of an apple.

"Just thinking about the last meal I ate off this table."

Her cheeks instantly flushed as her mouth hung open. I had the upper hand in my frustrating situation, so I might as well have a bit of fun.

"If you are going to leave your mouth hanging open like that, I can think of something to fill it with."

Her eyes instantly moved downward before snapping back to my face. She was so easily flustered, and I enjoyed it. Perhaps being trapped here wasn't so bad after all.

"Eat your breakfast," she snapped as she took another bite of apple. "We have things to do."

I kept my gaze locked on her as I grabbed a muffin from the table and took a bite. She was trying to act as if I did not affect her, but I could see that I did. Her cheeks and chest were flushed, she kept squeezing her thighs together, and she continuously shifted under my gaze. This woman was remarkable in every imaginable way. I didn't know how today would go or really much of anything, to be honest. One thing I knew for sure, my heart beat for her alone. And until it stopped beating, I wanted to savor every second of her, every taste she had to offer, and every moment in between.

Chapter 30

It had taken all morning to get Egon adjusted enough to go outside. I could still hear him grumbling under his breath as we made our way to the center of town. His gaze still had to be fixed on the ground, but at least he could move about again.

The rebels had already gathered. The crowd parted to let us through. Maddie and Garrett were already waiting for us in the center.

"Fun night?" Garrett asked, wearing a hat that was too big.

I looked at Maddie, who rolled her eyes and began shaking her head.

"Delicious."

I whipped around to where Egon stood. He was still looking down, but I could see the smirk on his face. I wanted to slap him, but forced myself to take a deep breath and focus. Garrett was laughing loudly until Maddie hit him in the chest.

"They're ready," Maddie assured me in a hushed tone as she motioned her head towards the rebels. "They just need you to tell them the plan."

I thanked her quietly and stepped forward. The crowd was silent as I looked around at their faces. The fear that had been there before was gone. It was now replaced with determination and hope.

"Today we end this," I said loudly. "We have a plan, and if we all stick to it, the Underdark will be free tonight!"

A roar of applause erupted. I looked around, trying to hide my surprise. I hadn't even told them the plan, and they were already praising me like the fight was already won. I held up a hand, and they fell silent once more.

"Those who can fight will be divided up into three groups," I continued. "Each group will be assigned a tunnel to sneak into the Underdark. Once inside, your task is to kill as many guards as you see and spare innocent lives who do not pose a threat."

I looked around, letting my words sink in. After just a moment, I could see in their expressions that they had questions, maybe even doubts.

"I will be heading in with a small group through a separate tunnel," I explained. "It leads straight into the snake's den. With the soldiers and guards all busy trying to stop the invasion from the tunnels, we will kill Blaylin."

The crowd cheered again, this time with less enthusiasm. I had just told them that they were bait, the distraction. There was no way to dress it up pretty, so I didn't try.

"I know we won't all make it to see the end of this fight." A few heads dropped, but I continued. "We must remember that this fight is not about us but about the future we are trying to save. And for that, we must be willing to risk everything. If we are not, then we are destined to lose everything we hold dear."

I watched as the people began to perk up. They began nodding in agreement as they nudged each other. It started as a soft murmur, and then the applause was like a roar. Egon stepped forward, gripped my wrist, and thrust our hands up to the sky. The roar of applause only grew louder as he slowly turned us in a circle for everyone to see.

Once we had turned towards everyone, he lowered my arm and stepped forward. "You all have an assignment," he bellowed. "I suggest you find out what it is and move to your location. We are leaving in an hour. Do not bother taking what you won't need. We will be spending one night in the tunnels before we breach the city. This will not be a long fight, but it will be brutal. Weapons and first aid will be your friends."

With that, everyone began to scatter. I watched as they formed groups around the pieces of parchment that Maddie had tacked up. No one complained as they found their assignment and went off to gather their supplies.

"They all are just acting like I've been here the entire time," I said softly. "I expected at least some of them to speak up or say I was unfit to lead."

"That's the thing about rebels," Maddie smiled. "You may have been gone, but they all knew your mother and about her mission. I'm sure she told them that if anything happened to her, you would be the one to finish it."

"So, they put up with Nyla because they were waiting for me?" I gasped, looking back at the people. "Why?"

No one answered as the groups continued to find their assignments and leave. Thoughts swirled through my head as I tried to process everything. Just a few weeks ago, I was fighting to survive, and now I was leading a rebel army. I had people journey all the way here from a city I've never heard of to help me take my place. A town full of people ready to follow my orders and die for the cause if necessary.

"They believe in it," I said, causing Maddie to smile. "They believe in what we are trying to do."

"Sounds about right," Garrett laughed. "That's what makes rebels so dangerous. They all believe in what they are doing and are willing to fight for it." The last of the people had walked off, leaving the four of us alone. "Is that what happened in your city?" I asked. Maddie had told me a little about where they were from, but I felt I needed to know. Perhaps knowing what they had been through would help me.

"Pretty much," Maddie nodded. "Liz's grandmother started the rebellion. She wanted to help other MUTS avoid being used by the governors. She planted the seeds, our parents built Twain, and really got things underway. Then, they were killed, Liz had her memories stolen, and Calix.... Well, without her, he lost the will to fight."

"Yet, we all stood by him and waited for our queen to return to us," Maddie continued. "It took seven years, but she came home. Her memory came back in flashes at first, but the governors made one crucial mistake that brought them all back."

"What was that?" I asked, a lump forming in my throat.

Maddie looked down, her eyes filling with tears.

"They murdered her grandmother," Garrett answered. "They sent her to Twain, and Elizabeth watched as she was burned alive. Just like they did to her and Cal's parents."

"They...." I couldn't bring myself to repeat it.

"You know the worst part?" Maddie asked, regaining her composure. "The bitch behind it all was actually Liz's grandmother, on her mother's side."

"Lilith?" Egon asked, his voice deep and gravely. "Was her name Lilith?"

Maddie nodded as she eyed Egon carefully. Even I was surprised that he would know the woman's name.

"Her husband, Samual, was my father," Egon explained. "He traded me away after Lilith killed my mother. That's how I ended up here."

"Shit," Garrett gasped. "Samuel was your father? That bastard has been missing. Liz would give anything to have him meet his end."

I watched as Egon's hands clenched at his sides. "He's dead," he replied. "I killed him myself when he showed up here asking for Blaylin to take him in."

Everyone was silent as Egon's words settled in around us. Things were bigger than any of us ever realized, and they had gone full circle. The last known enemy of The Union was dead, killed here by his son.

"The network?" I asked, shattering the silence. "What is the rebel network?"

"We just learned about that ourselves," Garrett sighed. "Turns out, years ago, the rebels in Twain sent out people to look for other cities. They didn't believe a word the governors said, not even that we were the last civilization left. Turns out, they were right. The scouts found four other cities, including this one."

"They knew that a fight was coming and wanted to be able to provide aid to each other if necessary," Maddie spoke up. "It took us a while to decipher it, but they set up Morse code communication. Very primitive yet effective. When we finally cracked into it, we saw your mother's message. Liz asked us to come here and check this out and help where we could."

"Why?" I asked before I could stop myself. "Why here and not the other three cities?"

"Only two of the others are on the network," Maddie explained. "The other one is cut off, and we have no idea why. Liz also sent people to the other two to check things out. It's not entirely selfless. Yes, we want to help, but she believes something bigger is at play. Something that may require us to come together to keep the freedom we fought so hard to earn."

"Maybe we should wait a bit longer to melt down that pickaxe," I said as I turned to Egon. "Our fighting may not be over once Blaylin is dead."

Chapter 31

An hour later, things were moving quickly. Everyone had gathered their supplies and was waiting at the entrance to the tunnels. Egon had left with Garrett after the meeting, and I hadn't seen him since. Spotting him just inside the entrance, I breathed a sigh of relief. As I approached, I couldn't help but notice that everyone was smiling at me with bright, smiling faces. It was unnerving, considering we were about to get into a battle.

"What's going on with them?" I asked as I reached Egon.

My heart began to thunder in my chest as he gave me the same nervous yet excited smile he used to when we were kids. I watched with wide eyes as he lowered down to one knee and took my hand.

"Bridget," he said with a slight tremor to his voice. "I have been yours since we were kids. I don't want to wait until the fighting is done to make you mine. So..."

I held my breath as he reached into his pocket, pulling out two silver rings.

"Instead of waiting to melt down my pickaxe, I got these. Then we can have each other, and I can use it to defend you until my last breath."

Everyone around us was silent, and I forgot they were there. Instead, my eyes were locked with Egon's. The face most people knew as a monster's, I saw the man. I could see his love and devotion to me in his dark brown eyes as he looked up at me.

"I am yours," I smiled down at him. "I always have been."

"Is that a yes?" Garrett asked, looking more nervous than anyone else.

"Yes," I laughed.

Egon erupted from his seat, pulled me into his arms, and kissed me. As the kiss ended, he pressed his forehead to mine.

"Garrett and Maddie said they would help us to the ceremony as they did," he explained.

It made sense that he had found another way. In The Underdark, a marriage required paperwork, credits, and a year waiting period. They viewed marriage as nothing but a transaction, just like everything else.

"Let's do this," I grinned up at him.

Egon wasted no time as he took my hand and turned to Garrett and Maddie. "We're ready."

Gone was the murderous tough guy, and in his place was a man overwhelmed with excitement.

"Bridgett?" Garrett's voice cut through my thoughts, drawing me to him. To my surprise, he was holding a small knife out to me. I had been so distracted that I hadn't heard a word he had said.

"It's alright," Egon assured me as he took the knife from Garrett and pressed it into my hand. "Just deep enough to leave a scar."

He held out his hand, and I looked at him, confused. Maddie caught my attention, pointing to her ring finger. Her ring was gone, and I could see two letters scarred into her skin, GM. I looked back at Egon and took a steadying breath. Carefully, I pressed the tip of the knife into his skin and carved my initials. When I finished, Garrett handed him a cup of water, and Egon washed the blood away and held out his hand to me once more. I took the ring from Maddie and slid it over his freshly cut finger. He was mine, forever marked as such.

Garrett rinsed the knife and handed it back to Egon. Now it was my turn to become his. I held out my hand and watched as he gently cut into my finger. The pain was more irritating, and I held still as he worked. When he finished, he rinsed where his initials were now carved and then slid the band on my finger. Now, I was forever marked as his.

Some people may have found it suffocating to be marked in such a way. I, however, did not share this sentiment. Although I had never heard of this marriage ritual, I found myself appreciating it. It wasn't someone claiming you. It was more than that. I gave myself to him and him to me. Rings could be removed, but these marks would remain. Its permanence ran deep in my soul, and I knew I was finally complete.

"Now, by the lack of power I have," Garrett announced loudly, "I pronounce you married!"

The crowd immediately erupted in cheers as Egon pulled me into his arms. His kiss was soft and tender, a side of him that I found I enjoyed just as much as the hard and ruthless.

"Unfortunately, the wedding night will have to wait," Maddie teased when we pulled apart. "We have a fight to get to."

Egon took my hand with a sly grin and turned back to the crowd. I wasn't sure what he had planned for our wedding night. However, I knew without a doubt that it would be diabolical, and I had to resist taking him back to the hut that very moment. I forced myself to look at the crowd that was full of smiles, pride, and determination.

Our ceremony made me almost forget that we were leaving to lay siege to The Underdark. They were all looking to me, waiting for something inspirational to carry them into battle. Words escaped me as I looked out at their faces. Their cheering slowly died down, and the silence began to creep in.

"We deserve this," I heard myself speak. "Happiness. Not just myself, but all of us. Free to live without a tyrant constantly crushing us under their boot. Today, we remind them that it's not the ruler that holds the power but the people. We are the ones who ensure they have their luxuries and their power. Our loyalty has been used to beat us down. Today, we take the power back and watch their world crumble around them!"

The tension was thick as everyone began nodding in agreement. My words had resonated with them, and even I felt empowered. Beside me, Egon squeezed my hand. There was something more needed. Something less polished and political. Something more for me.

"So, let's go kick their fucking asses!" I yelled.

Everyone yelled in agreement and began marching into the tunnels. There was no going back now. The rebellion had started, and for some reason, they were all trusting me to lead them to victory.

"Hell of a speech," Maddie grinned as the last of the rebels walked past us. "Can honestly say I've never heard a leader use that phrasing to fire up the troops."

"I liked it," Garrett laughed. "I don't even live here, and I'm inspired to make them pay for the suffering I've endured."

I laughed, and any worry or embarrassment I felt melted away. "Well, let's get to it," I said as I started walking into the tunnels.

"We've got some asses to kick," Egon said in a gruff voice, but I could see the hint of a smile tugging at the corners of his mouth.

Chapter 32

Our path was different from the others' paths. They were heading to strategic points on the upper levels to draw the soldiers away. In truth, they were nothing but bait, but for Bridgett, they took the role willingly. I hadn't had time to see if there were any real fighters among them. In truth, we had a lot riding on the hope that they could keep the soldiers busy while we cut off the snake's head.

I looked over at Bridgett, her gentle features just visible in the low light. Her words had sounded perfect, just like a noble leader. But the ending was what made it perfect. It was all her, unfiltered and real. I twisted the ring on my finger, the fresh cut beneath it burning slightly. I didn't want either of us to go into this with any doubts or regrets. Hearing her say last night that she wasn't sure if I wanted a future with her was the push I needed. The moment she said yes, my final wall came tumbling down.

No matter what happened, nothing could tear us apart. We belonged to each other, and now we both knew, without a question, that what was between us was forever. I was done being the murderous captain. That part of me died the moment I gave myself to her. Now, I would only fight or kill for her. I would protect her over everything else in this world.

"This is it," Maddie yelled over her shoulder. "Brace 2257."

I looked up at the cross beam and saw that she was right, we had arrived. I moved forward and joined Garrett at the side pole. At first glance, it looked just like another support brace. But if a person were paying attention, they would see that this one was placed too close. All of the beams were evenly spread to distribute the weight and conserve materials. This one was in the wrong spot. I reached forward to help Garrett with the brace when it moved and was tossed aside before I even touched it. I looked at him in surprise. Strength, the one gift that Blaylin had punished me for not possessing.

"You let me beat you," I said in a low voice.

Garrett looked at me, a boyish grin on his face. "I did."

"Why?" I asked the question before I could stop myself. It didn't matter, not really. Yet, I still had to know.

"You weren't fighting me," Garrett replied. "Not really. You were fighting for her and trying to protect her when you had been unable since she was taken. I knew we had bigger fights ahead, and that she needed you to keep your head. So, I took the beating."

"I could have killed you," I growled, shaking my head.

Garrett let out a hearty laugh that reverberated in the tunnel. "No, you wouldn't have. She would have stopped you."

"She did stop me!" I insisted.

"Not Bridgett," Garrett corrected as he looked past me. I turned to see Maddie and Bridgett talking, their conversation too soft for me to hear. "True love is rare." Garrett pulled my attention back to him.
"And my little siren can be quite

persuasive, even deadly if needed."

I felt an understanding wash over me. I had lived too long under Blaylin's control. I always assumed the worst in people, believing the few I had met that were decent were rare. I thought of the rebels marching through the tunnels, Maddie and Garrett traveling such a great distance to help strangers, and I realized that I was wrong. Evil was louder, more dominating, but it was not the way of most people. Most people had good hearts and, given the chance, would do good things.

Turning, I looked back at Bridgett as she was laughing at something Maddie had said. It was a lesson that I learned at a young age and let myself forget. Bridgett had shown me that good can be found in the darkest of places. She had seen past the monster and brought out the good in me.

"If something were to happen," I said without looking away from her. "I need you to be there for her. Don't let her give up."

"Nothing will happen," Garrett assured me. "In my experience, it takes more than a little rebellion to tear a love like yours apart."

I hoped that he was right. Still, I felt that he would be there for her if I died. She was all that mattered, and I would do whatever it took to give her the life she deserved.

"We should get some rest," Bridgett said as she and Maddie joined us. "We still have several hours before the others will make their grand entrance."

I nodded in agreement and sank against the wall. Bridgett followed, and I pulled her close to me, her head resting on my chest. I glanced up and saw that Maddie and Garrett were in the same position. There was no need for a watch. We were in a forgotten tunnel, preparing for the four of us to attempt to assassinate the president. Who else would be wandering these tunnels?

Chapter 33

Despite being in a tunnel, preparing to kill Blaylin, sleep had come easily. The sound of Egon's heart lulled me straight to sleep. When I woke, it wasn't a gentle waking. It was a feeling that pulled me out of my rest. A feeling of someone watching me. Slowly, I looked around and saw that the others were still asleep. Egon's arms were still wrapped around me, holding me close to him.

I was just about to close my eyes once more when something caught my attention just outside the tunnel. We had moved into the hidden tunnel, but something stood just outside the entrance. My body tensed as I strained my eyes, willing myself to see through the darkness.

"Please, don't wake them." Felix's voice came out barely above a whisper.

I shouldn't trust him, not after what I learned about him being involved with Nyla. Still, I wanted to believe that he was my friend. To give him a chance to explain.

Carefully, I slipped out of Egon's arms. He groaned in his sleep and then settled. I moved through the tunnel silently and found Felix waiting for me. Egon hadn't exaggerated what had happened in the speakeasy. Felix's face was still bruised, and the cuts were still healing.

"What are you doing here?" I breathed. "How did you know about this place?"

"There's no time," Felix sighed. "I'll explain everything, I promise. But we need to go."

"Go?" I laughed in annoyance. "We are a few hours away from the fight that will bring Blaylin to his knees. You really think I'm going to leave and follow you?"

Felix looked hurt. Vulnerability was not something I had ever seen on his face before. It looked out of place, and my stomach twisted into a knot.

"How did you get here?" I asked firmly as I took a step closer to him. "Taylor wouldn't have let you go."

Felix looked past me at those who were still sleeping. "He didn't," he admitted. "They were taken yesterday. The soldiers didn't see where he had me tied up behind the bar."

My heart froze in my chest: Ginny, Taylor, the girls. Soldiers took them. Blaylin had made the first move a day earlier and had gone for the throat. When we rushed his manor, he would use them as leverage. He knew when to strike and didn't hesitate.

"I fought the damn ropes until I finally slipped them," Felix said, holding out his wrists. Even in the dim light, I could see the flesh was torn from ripping himself free. "I went into the tunnels to find you. I came across an army and hid. Then I saw you heading this way. I had to wait until I could talk to you alone."

His words echoed in my mind, but I could only focus on the fact that Blaylin had them. My family had been captured and possibly tortured by that son of a bitch.

"What good would leaving do?" I snarled. "The only way to help them is to finish this."

"He knows where they are." Maddie's soft voice caused me to jump. I turned to see her standing directly behind me. "His tension woke me up," she shrugged. He's telling the truth, at least about this."

I looked back at Felix and could see that Maddie was right.

"Blaylin is impatient," Felix sighed. He had them taken to the incinerator. At lights on, he is going to have them thrown in one at a time. He says their screams will stop anyone else in The Underdark from rising against him."

"We need to wake..."

"No," Felix pleaded as he grabbed my wrist. His gaze landed on my ring and then slowly made its way to my face. "No offense, but they aren't good at blending in. If we are spotted before we reach them, they will be killed. We need to do this quietly."

I looked back at Egon, his arms draped over his chest. I should still be there, savoring every moment I could with my husband. But I knew I couldn't leave my family to die.

"We have to get them before dawn," I said sternly. "Regardless of whether we move or not, the rebels will begin their attack right on time."

"When's that?" Felix asked, his voice shaking.

"One hour after lights on," Maddie answered. "At the shift change."

"For the most chaos and confusion," Felix nodded.

"I have to be back before then."

Felix looked at me and nodded. I could tell he wanted to argue, but he didn't.

"If he wakes before I get back, don't tell him who I left with," I said, turning to Maddie.

Maddie shook her head as she pulled a knife from her boot and began to carve into the wall. I looked toward the men, asleep, praying the scraping wouldn't wake them. I breathed a sigh of relief as the sound faded and they both stayed asleep.

"I'm coming with you," Maddie said as she returned her knife to her boot.

I looked at the wall and saw that she had carved a message.

BRB

"Be right back," Maddie explained. "Garrett will know what it means and that they should stay here. Leaving would risk them losing us if we returned and they are gone."

"Alright," I breathed. "Lead the way, Felix."

Chapter 34

Felix opened the hatch, and I followed him up into the speakeasy. Maddie followed up behind me, my silent shadow as we made our way through the tunnels. None of us had said anything as we walked, unthinkingly following Felix. I was glad that she insisted on coming with me. My trust in Felix was new and had already been shattered. In truth, I couldn't remember how or why we had welcomed him into our group. He just showed up, sat down, and became one of us.

That was my mistake. I knew better than to trust, especially someone like him, unthinkingly. That wasn't a mistake that I would make again—any hint that he was betraying me, and I would kill him myself.

Inside, I could see that Taylor and the others had been busy with cleanup. There were still piles of debris, but they had been pushed against the outer walls. Tables stood with their chairs surrounding them as if they were waiting for customers to arrive.

I glanced behind the bar as we walked and saw the chair that Felix had been tied to. The rope was still around the arms, coated thick with dried blood, more of which was pooled on the ground.

I looked at Felix's wrists and could see that the wounds still hadn't fully closed. He was telling the truth about how he escaped. The pain must have been near unbearable, but he did it to get to me. To give me a chance to save my family.

"We need to bandage your wrists," I said.

"Plan on it," Felix muttered, his normal arrogance still missing from his words. "The tunnel isn't the only thing in this place that Taylor was clueless about."

I glanced back at Maddie as we followed Felix to where the stereo was set up. I watched as he walked behind it and placed his hands on the wall. I couldn't help the surprised gasp that escaped me as he pressed, and the wall gave. I watched as he pushed open a hidden door and stepped inside.

"Are you coming?" Felix called from inside.

Cautiously, I walked towards the opening, Maddie right behind me. Inside, soft light illuminated the room. The walls were lined with shelves and racks of weapons. In one corner was a small cot and a few rations.

"What is this?" I asked as I stepped in.

"Safe room," Felix answered. "Your mother had it made after she escaped. It was used to hide rebels until they were moved to the town."

"And to store weapons," Maddie added as she motioned to them.

"And that," Felix nodded as he grabbed a first aid kit and opened it.

Stepping forward, I took it from his hands. "Let me," I insisted. Felix looked at me cautiously before holding out his wrists. Carefully, I cleaned them as best I could and wrapped them in thick, white bandages. "How does Taylor not know about this place?" I asked as I finished. "And how do you?"

"He was young when his father was killed for helping the rebels," Felix answered. "This place was abandoned for a long time after that. The shine just sitting and the rebellion outside forgotten."

It finally made sense. Taylor always said he had to reopen the speakeasy because Blaylin was punishing him. He never said what he did to earn the punishment, but now I figured that was because he didn't know. Killing Taylor's father hadn't been enough. Blaylin was punishing Taylor for things he had no clue about.

"As far as me, I was born into this fight much like you," he continued. "My mother was a point of contact in The Underdark. When she was killed, I sent a message to the outside like I had seen her do a thousand times. I took over her duties, including keeping an eye on you."

My mind felt numb, but I remained calm. "But you kept reporting to them that I wasn't ready to fight. You knew I wanted Blaylin dead."

"I also knew the truth about Nyla," Felix countered. "You needed to be ready to learn about not only who your parents were, but strong enough to face the woman who murdered your mother."

Felix knew the truth. He had been protecting me in his own way.

"You should arm yourself," Felix said as he stood and began strapping weapons on. "We are going to need more than strong feelings to win this fight. I'm surprised you didn't do it before, but I guess you were always the dim bulb."

"Hey!" I blurted out. He looked at me, an eyebrow raised, waiting for my defense. None came, so I instead moved to the shelves and began selecting weapons. Why hadn't I taken the time to get weapons before? It wasn't like I didn't know how to use them. As a child, Blaylin had demanded that I be trained with all sorts of weapons.

There was my answer. The last time I had held a weapon was in one of my training sessions. In rejecting everything Blaylin was, I had refused to touch one after he banished me. I hadn't even realized how deeply it was ingrained until now.

"I suggest knives," Felix said, tucking another knife into his belt. "The guns haven't been maintained, and their noise level is dangerous under the best of circumstances. If we cause a cave-in...well."

I nodded in agreement as I pulled several small knives from the racks and began tucking them onto my person. Just as we were about to leave, I spotted a blade that seemed out of place. It was the size of a small sword, thin and light. The hilt was ornate, its gold rings glinting. At the end of the hilt was a hawk with its wings spread. It looked as if it had been carved out of coal.

"Fancy for a rebel stash," Maddie noted as she followed my gaze.

"It was your mother's," Felix said, not looking up. "It had been handed down through the women in your family. She kept it here, swearing she would use it to kill Blaylin."

That was all I needed to hear. I grabbed the sword. It was light as a feather and fit perfectly in my hand. I tucked it into my belt, the blade sticking out behind me.

She was the first to stand up to that bastard, and I would see to it that she got her revenge.

Chapter 35

The tunnels were still dark as we crept out of the speakeasy. The red light illuminated the area around us in an eerie glow. I used to find it comforting, but tonight it felt ominous.

"Stay close," Felix whispered as he flicked on a flashlight. He kept it on the ground, just enough to keep us from tripping on the uneven stone but not enough to see ahead.

My anxiety grew the longer we walked. I had no idea what time it was, but I could feel that this was taking too long. "We need to move faster," I whispered.

Felix didn't answer but instead held up a hand to silence me. I was about to yell at him when a voice in the distance rang out.

"The little one last," a deep, burly voice echoed. "His screams will haunt them longer."

"Don't you touch her!" Taylor yelled back, anger and desperation dripping from his voice.

Felix looked back at me and mouthed, "Stay Close." I placed my hand on his shoulder and felt Maddie do the same to me. The next moment, the light disappeared. Slowly, I allowed Felix to lead us through the dark, the voices growing louder. I could hear the girls sobbing as Taylor and Ginny cursed the soldiers.

Felix came to a stop. We were outside the incinerator door. I could see the light squeezing out through the cracks around the door. Felix bent down, looking through one at what was going on. When he stood, he tapped my hand ten times. I did the same to Maddies, hoping she understood as I swallowed hard. Ten soldiers. It had been years since I last fought with a weapon. Now, I was about to go into a fight outnumbered, with lives on the line. No pressure.

Felix shrugged my hand off his shoulder, which I took as a sign that it was time. I pulled a dagger from my belt and felt Maddie release me and prepare herself. I wouldn't use the sword unless I had to; I would save it for Blaylin.

In the next moment, Felix kicked the door open. The light was blinding, but I moved instinctively forward. As my eyes adjusted, I could see that our attack had taken everyone by surprise. Felix moved like water, slicing his blade across two of the soldiers' throats before they had even drawn their swords. Maddie rushed past me, leaping onto the back of another and burying her blade just below his skull. As he fell to the ground, she stood gracefully and pulled back her dagger. An arc of red blood sprayed as she did, looking somehow magical in the firelight.

"Bridgett!" Ginny's scream brought me back to the present just as a large arm wrapped around my chest. I moved quickly, driving my dagger into the beefy forearm. The soldier let out a blood-curdling scream and pulled back. I spun, raising the dagger as I did, and slid it cleanly across his throat. He gasped at me as he fell to his knees and then collapsed.

The other soldiers were ready now as they moved to attack. Felix continued to flow between them, dodging a sword and killing two more. Out of the corner of my eye, I could see that Maddie was using her gift on three of the others. They had lowered their weapons and appeared to be flirting with her. Felix was already moving into position behind them, his knife dripping with blood. It would only be moments before they were all dead.

My eyes locked on the last soldier. He was holding Patty with a knife to her throat. I could feel the fear radiating off the little girl as she looked at me with a tear-stained face. My first instinct was to rush him and drive my blade into his eye. I held back, knowing there was a good chance that it would end with Patty's blood being spilled.

"Let her go," I growled, stepping forward.

"No," he shot back. "Take one more step, and I will end her!"

Suddenly, I felt everyone's fear. It was strong enough that part of me wanted to fall to the ground and cry myself. The only thing that kept me strong was knowing the fear wasn't entirely mine, and I was the only one who could stop it. I got an idea. It probably wouldn't work, but there was no harm in trying. The worst that would happen is the soldier would think we were in some awkward stare-off. I could project my feelings onto others. If I were feeling their fear, perhaps I could project it onto the soldier.

I stared intently at the soldier, willing the emotions to flow through me and into him. The emotions grew strong, as if I were forcing myself to absorb more rather than project. The fear was becoming overwhelming, and I was about to give up when it happened. It felt like a damn opening up as they began to flood out of me. I still felt them all, but it was only briefly as they passed through me.

The soldier's hand began to tremble, and his sword clattered to the ground. Patty, being the smart shit she was, sensed his weakness and fought hard. She fell to the ground as he released her and crawled over to Taylor. Taylor immediately scooped her into his arms. The soldier was falling apart, his fear driving him slowly insane.

I kept the emotions flowing, tapping into others that lay just beyond the surface. Pain became my primary focus. He had caused much of it, and I wanted him to feel every ounce of it. I could feel my gift reaching out beyond the room, into The Underdark. The soldier was screaming now, his hands clung to his head as he collapsed.

"Bridgett," Maddie said gently as she placed a hand on my shoulder.

Breaking the connection, I felt exhausted. I felt something warm running down my face. I reached up and wiped away blood. It was streaming out of my nose. The soldier let out a groan, drawing my attention back to him. Felix ran forward and ended the soldiers' life.

"Sit," Maddie instructed me. I listened and leaned against the stone wall. I took deep breaths as I looked over at my family.

They were huddled together, looking at me with concern.

"Accessing a new part of the gift takes practice," Maddie explained. "It's like a muscle you have to build up strength in."

"I don't have time," I replied, wiping my face clean. My breathing returned to normal.

"Pushing it too fast can kill you," she continued.

I could already feel strength returning to my body. Maddie was probably right. Yet I suddenly knew exactly how to use my gift. I would avoid it, saving what little strength remained for Blaylin. He would feel the pain and suffering he inflicted upon everyone in this city.

"I'm okay," I breathed to Maddie. "I won't do it again."

The lie tasted bitter on my tongue. The look on Maddie's face told me she didn't believe me, but wasn't going to argue.

Chapter 36

We made our way through the dark tunnels, the others joining us, as we made our way back to the speakeasy. Maddie and I needed to return to the tunnels, and there the others could lock themselves in the safe room. We were approaching the glowing red light when the bright overhead lights turned on.

"Shit!" I cursed. "We will never make it back in time!"

"Not through the hidden tunnel," Felix agreed. "But the elevator would get you there faster."

I thought of Egon. He was waiting in that tunnel, probably being physically restrained by Garrett. Knowing him, his rage would compel him to finish Blaylin when the time came, even if I hadn't returned. He wouldn't be able to hold back. He couldn't do this alone; he needed me.

Walking through the city was risky. After all, I was banned from the upper level.

"Let's go," Maddie urged. "I can keep them from looking at you."

"This has to end," Taylor encouraged.

I hadn't noticed, but he was injured, probably from fighting the soldiers when they were taken. I had thought he would be able to defend everyone if the soldiers found them, but now I doubted it. He couldn't stand on his own, leaning heavily on his daughters. I turned to Felix, knowing that my decision was a risk but the only option I had.

"You go with them," I said sternly. "You keep them safe."

"I would be of better use..."

"I need you to keep them safe," I interrupted him. "I'm trusting you, Felix. I'm trusting you to keep my family safe."

His eyes widened for a moment as the weight of my words sank in. "I will protect them with my life," he finally swore.

"Thank you," I said with sincerity.

Felix took a step towards Taylor, shifting his weight from the girls to himself. I watched as they all rushed towards the speakeasy. They would be safe; they had to be.

"Let's go," I said to Maddie as I turned and headed down the tunnel. I began to run, knowing that time was not on our side. The sound of Maddie's boots hitting the stone floor behind me told me she was keeping my pace.

We reached the elevator within minutes. The metal doors slammed shut as I pushed for us to be taken to the top level. My stomach instantly tightened into a knot as we began to rise. Reaching the top level was the easy part. Everything after that would be difficult.

"It's going to be fine," Maddie assured me. Her fiery red hair was a tussled mess from the fighting we had already done. Our plan of even making it to the president's cavern rested on her ability to keep their eyes on her, preferably in a good way.

"Don't worry," she smiled, noticing my gaze. "I could be covered in literal shit, and my gift would make them all smitten."

I trusted her. After all, I had seen the soldiers in the incinerator stop fighting to get her attention.

The time for talking ended as the elevator lurched to a sudden stop. I opened the metal doors and cautiously stepped out. The tunnels were still empty. Within the next few minutes, the soldiers would begin making their way through for the shift change, and shortly after, the city would come alive. We needed to move quickly. If we weren't to the president's cavern before the rebels made their move, things would get messy.

"This way," I whispered as I led Maddie through the tunnels. I could see Maddie looking around at the stores as we walked. "Just like home," she sighed.

"What do you mean?"

The conversation was dangerous, but I was desperate for anything else to think about. I kept picturing Egon taking on Blaylin without me. I couldn't lose him.

"Those in power live in luxury while those without it live in squalor," Maddie explained. "It was the same way back in The Union."

"I'm pretty sure it's that way everywhere," I replied, slipping down another tunnel. We were getting close.

"It doesn't have to be," Maddie said as she continued to follow. "The Union is different now. Elizabeth and Calix had made things equal, brought us all together."

Ahead, I could see the entrance to the President's cavern. There would be guards, though I couldn't see them from where we stood.

"Bridgett," Maddie said firmly as she gripped my arm and forced me to stop. "It's important you know that things don't have to be this way."

"Why?" I snapped. "All I want to do is kill Blaylin. After that, the people can do as they want. It's of no concern to me."

Maddie looked taken aback, but her face remained stern.

"Whether you like it or not, you are the heir," she said firmly. "When Blaylin is dead, it will be up to you to lead these people."

I felt anger rising inside me. I didn't want to be in charge. I just wanted Blaylin dead and to live my life free with Egon. Just because the son of a bitch was my father and my mother chose to lead a rebellion, I had to take over everything now!

"I don't want it," I snarled.

"Then there's no point in going any further," Maddie sighed. "People without leadership are dangerous. Another power struggle will divide them even further. Blaylin may be insane, but at least he is some form of leadership. The devil they know."

"We don't have time for this! We can figure out what comes next after he's dead!"

My heart froze as the sound of boots began to echo; the shift change was beginning. "Maddie," I pleaded. "We have to go."

Maddie eyed me slowly and then nodded. She walked ahead of me just as the soldiers began to fill the tunnel. Just as she promised, they all parted and looked at her like she was a goddess, paying no attention to me. We had just reached the entrance to the President's cavern when the sounds of fighting began to echo all around us. The rebels were making their move.

Inside the cavern, the soldiers began rushing about, presumably heading down different tunnels to join the fight. I watch from our hiding spot as Blaylin strolled out of the manor across the green grass. He stopped by the fountain, staring into the water. From where we were, it looked like he was already bored with the situation. I went to move forward just as Maddie grabbed my arm.

"Wait," she mouthed.

I settled back in, never taking my eyes off Blaylin. I knew what we were waiting for. Egon and Garrett had yet to arrive. If they didn't come, we were at a severe disadvantage.

Chapter 37

"How much longer do you plan on hiding in the shadows?" Blaylin's voice was calm as it echoed around the cavern.

Maddie and I locked eyes, silently exchanging our surprise. Maddie shook her head, signaling that she didn't think we should move.

"If you're waiting for your men, they are already here," Blaylin continued. "Arrived just before the alarms went off."

This couldn't be happening. The guys wouldn't have moved early. I couldn't believe it. I could see them moving without us, sticking to the plan, but not early.

Maddie closed her eyes, and I saw a silent tear slip down her cheek. When she opened them, I reached out with my gift and could feel her pain. Reaching a little further, I could feel their pain. I felt like I was being crushed under the weight of the cavern, being ground into the stone.

"Let them go!" I yelled, jumping out of the shadows and stepping into the cavern.

Blaylin was facing me, a smile tugging at his lips. From where I stood, I could see both Egon and Garrett, their bodies partially pressed into the ground. Maddie joined me, her dagger already drawn, rage rolling off her waves.

"Looks like I traded for the wrong Union child," Blaylin said as he glanced at Garrett. "It was quite impressive to watch him tear through my men like they were nothing. Too bad all that strength does him no good when there's nothing to use it on."

Garrett was pressing into the ground, the struggle of trying to push against Blaylin's gift showing on his face. My eyes moved to Egon, and I was surprised to see that he seemed to have accepted his fate. There was no indication that he was struggling. In fact, looking at Blaylin, I could see that Egon hadn't used his gift. There was no sign of blood anywhere on Blaylin's skin.

"I propose a deal," Blaylin said, turning back to Maddie and me. "One child. You and Egon give me one child, and I will allow all of you to return to the surface on the condition that you never return."

"You're insane!" I fired back, my hand tightening around the sword's hilt. "All of this just to have a blood heir to continue your legacy! Is your ego really that delicate?!"

Blaylin let out a hearty laugh. Once he recovered, he looked at me with a more serious expression. "I assure you, Ego has nothing to do with it, daughter. It's the rules of this place, this life. Only one of our bloodlines can rule. You are not eligible due to your... insufficient standing. Without a male blood heir, the Underdark will end the moment I die."

Now he was speaking in riddles, and I had no patience for it. Knowing Blaylin as I did, there was some truth behind his ramblings; I just needed to know how much before I killed him. Maddie's words suddenly echoed in my mind, about me needing to take over once he was dead. I glanced at her, but her stare was locked on

Blaylin, bloodlust in her glare. Had she known about what he was saying? Did I have to take over because I was Blaylin's child, or would the Underdark be destroyed?

"You don't need a male heir," I yelled back as I drew my sword. "As long as I live, the Underdark will survive."

Blaylin's face drained of color, and I knew that my assumption had been correct. Whatever rules he was talking about did not actually say there had to be a male heir. That part of his story was his ego not wanting to give power to a woman. Something about that would make killing him even more enjoyable.

"You little shit!" Blaylin yelled, and I felt the pressure weigh down on my shoulders. I knew instantly that he was using his gift. Soon, I would be pinned to the ground just like Egon and Garrett. "I simply need your body as the incubator. There's no need for you to be functioning or even survive after."

My eyes broke away from him as I felt my knees begin to buckle. I had wanted to avenge my mother, but instead I was going to be forced into the same position she was. Strapped to a table, forced to be impregnated and have a child, and then handed over to him.

"Aghhh!"

Blaylin's screams cut through my thoughts, and the pressure immediately disappeared. I whipped my head up and could see the blood running from his eyes, nose, and ears in thick red streams. Behind him, Egon and Garrett were still pinned to the ground; his gift had not released on them. It must have been too much for him to focus on all of us, and he was bleeding out.

"You want to know why your regime failed?" I asked firmly as I took several steps forward. "Why will you die at the hands of the children you raised?"

Blaylin didn't answer as he frantically wiped at the blood, trying to will it to stop.

"Let me show you."

With that, I allowed all of the hurt and pain he caused to flow through me and into him. I opened my reach, slowly adding in Egon's, Garrett's, Maddie's, and the staff of the manor. Blaylins' screams grew louder as he covered his ears, trying to keep the emotions out. It wasn't enough. I reached out further, my body trembling as all the hurt and pain flowed through me. The people of the Underdark suffered at his hand; he could feel it.

"Bridgett!" Maddie's voice sounded as if she were down a long tunnel. I could feel the blood running down my face, but I refused to stop. He was going to feel it all. He deserved to feel it all. I could feel my body was beyond exhaustion when something around me changed.

"Now!" Egon's voice rang out.

He and Garrett were on their feet, and Egon was holding Blayin from behind. Somehow, I knew exactly what he meant. I gripped my mother's sword and rushed the last few feet forward. The sword slid into his chest until the hilt was against his flesh. Blaylin looked up at me with surprise. He tried to speak, but instead, only a gurgling sound escaped as he choked on his own blood.

"Rot in hell!" I snarled as I pulled the sword out, and Egon dropped him to the ground.

"The fountain!" We all looked to see an older maid sprinting across the lawn just as the cavern began to shake. "There has to be an heir!" she shouted.

I tried to rush forward, but my body was done. I collapsed next to the fountain, cutting my hand on the sword as I fell. I gripped the edge, the blood flowing over the stone and into the clear, cool water. Egon was by my side in the next breath, pulling me up to sit on the ledge. We watched as my blood ran through the water, and the cavern stilled once again.

Looking back, the maid had collapsed but was smiling as tears ran down her face. I looked at Maddie, who gave me a knowing smirk.

"You knew," I gasped between heavy breaths.

"It's part of the fucked-up rules for each civilization," she nodded. "A blood heir always has to take control when the ruler dies, or the city will self-destruct. Elizabeth gave her blood unknowingly. Her grandmother saw to it that she would be the heir whether she liked it or not. She made us all promise not to do that if we found an heir. While she wouldn't change her decision to lead, she said everyone deserves the choice."

"Some choice," Egon breathed as he began to wrap my hand.

"But a choice nonetheless," Garrett grinned as he pulled Maddie into his arms.

Chapter 38

I woke in a soft bed with white sheets. The blood and coal dust had been washed away, and my clothes changed. I sat up with a start, looking around. I was alone in a room big enough for a family of five to live in comfortably. I was in the center of a gigantic bed. There was large, beautiful furniture and decorations throughout the room, but my brain refused to process them. I realized there was only one place I could be: the manor.

For a moment, I forgot about the fight and began to scramble to get out of bed. Before I managed to do more than push the sheets off, the door opened. I froze and looked at the door as Egon entered. I felt my body instantly relax as he grinned at me and strode across the room.

"Thinking about running away?" he asked as he sat on the edge of the bed.

I scooted closer to him, desperate to feel his touch. His arms wrapped around me and held me close. He had cleaned up but was still wearing his signature black shirt.

"The rebels!" I gasped, suddenly remembering the fights the rebels had started to draw the soldiers away.

"They're fine," Egon assured me. "Though you should probably just call them citizens now."

The silence settled back around us like a warm blanket. However, I was not known for enjoying calm or for not speaking my mind.

"Why did you go in early?" I blurted out as I smacked his chest. "And why did you wait to use your gift?"

Egon let out a slight laugh as he pulled me back to him. I loved that sound more than anything in the world.

"Garrett told me about the heir stipulation when we woke up, and you guys were gone," he explained. "I wanted to beat him to death for not saying something sooner, but then he explained about the choice. I knew you would resist if anyone tried to force you to take over, so I agreed to let you make the choice."

I leaned closer, listening to his heart thrum under my ear.

"I knew you would make it to the cavern before the fighting started," he continued. "You had to be the one to kill Blaylin; you needed that. We went in early to give him the upper hand. I waited until you were ready before acting."

"So, you did it all for me?" I asked softly.

"Everything I do is for you," he said as he kissed my hair and squeezed me tighter.

I wanted to stay like this, locked in this room with just him. Perhaps we could even have our wedding night. However, I had made a choice, and I would honor it.

"They are waiting when you are ready," Egon said softly.

Damn it, I had projected my emotions onto him again. As far as I could tell, he was the only one I couldn't control. That would make for an interesting life together.

"What if I fail?" I asked as fear crept up my throat.

I was good at taking care of myself, surviving. This was different. This was thousands of people looking to me for direction and to keep them all safe.

"I won't let you," Egon assured me as he released me and stood up. "We do this together."

Taking his hand, I stood up out of the bed. "Together," I echoed.

Egon led me out to the balcony. The lawn was crowded with dirty faces all looking up at me. There was a murmur of voices as I looked over all of them. Things had already changed in evident ways. The level colors were all mixed, all looking equally tired and scared.

"It's time for change," I said loudly, my voice echoing as everyone fell silent.

"Blaylin kept us separated and hidden underground. It is time for us to come together and rise."

Everyone looked around, and I could sense their doubt in my words.

"If you want to hear all the answers today, I don't have them," I admitted. "I can't promise everything will be perfect or easy. What I can promise is that I have no desire to rule you. I only want to help create a world where everyone has access to food and happiness."

I could feel their tension easing, and something else that made me smile: hope.

"The first step is accepting that the Underdark no longer exists," I continued. "We are now The Mountaineers. We don't just live on the mountains, but in them, we are the mountains!"

The crowd erupted with applause. For now, I could feel that they all believed me and were ready for the change. I felt my body tremble and grabbed Egon's arm for support. He gripped my shoulders and led me back inside to the bed.

"Rest," he instructed as he helped me lie down. "You pushed yourself too far. Your body is weak."

"But I want my wedding night," I pouted as my eyelids grew heavy.

"Not until you're rested," Egon said sternly as he pulled the blankets up. "I need you at full strength for what I have planned."

I felt my cheeks go red just as my eyes slid shut. The fight was over, but we had a hard road ahead of us. Words were easy and pretty, but I knew it wouldn't be easy. Not only did I have to restructure the city to make things equal, but I also needed to expand to the surface. Maddie and Garrett said there were other cities. Whatever or whoever set the rules had made the cavern shake and was still out there. Nothing would matter unless we were freed from that unknown source.

Epilogue

"Princess! The King requires your presence!"

Talia's voice rang through the heavy wooden door. I opened my eyes and saw that dawn was just on the horizon. That explained why Talia was calling from outside instead of coming in and demanding I get up. My loyal maid knew that I hated early mornings and could be a bit of a tyrant if awakened early.

"Is he serious?!" I called back, squeezing my eyes shut.

"Deadly!" she called back.

I was up, my eyes wide as saucers. That was our code word for I needed to stop playing around and get moving. Talia had only used it once before when my door was locked, and the castle was raided.

Throwing back the thick blankets, I jumped out of bed and grabbed my dress. I heard the door crack behind me as Talia stepped inside. I slipped out of my nightgown and allowed it to pool on the floor. Talia was by my side, helping me into the smooth silk dress. Once she had the purple waist sash tied, she fetched the matching shoes and helped me into them.

"Sit," she instructed as she motioned to my vanity.

Whatever was going on was serious, but my father's anger would only be greater if I showed up looking anything but royal. Talia's fingers worked quickly as she brushed and braided the sides of my hair, then tied the pieces together at the back of my head with a purple bow, pinning in a few purple flowers into the braid for elegance.

While she worked, I quickly applied light makeup, smoothing my eyes and filling in my lips. I always appreciated how Talia and I could work in complete silence and accomplish what took other ladies an hour in a matter of minutes. It helped that she had been my maid since I was born. She wasn't one to treat me like a princess.

She told me that she was there to help, not do everything for me. I was going to rule one day, and a ruler who didn't know how to even take care of themselves was useless. I took her teaching to heart and learned everything I could when my father didn't have me sitting like a china doll at court.

Talia and I finished at the same time. As she stepped back, I stood and followed her to the door. In the hall, Talia fell in behind me. To everyone else, she looked like a dutiful and silent maid. I hated that she had to hide the fire she possessed when others were around. That was something I would change when I took the crown.

The stone halls were cold as my clicking shoes guided us downstairs and into the throne room. There, on the throne, sat my father, the king. I walked smoothly up the center of the room. Soldiers and generals were everywhere, but I saw no signs that any of them had been in a battle.

"My king," I said as I gracefully bent into a deep bow.

"Rise, daughter." My father's voice was deep, and I could hear the anger behind the words.

It was more than that, though. It almost sounded as if he was afraid. Smoothing my dress as I stood, I looked him in the eye.

"Two of the cities have fallen and been reclaimed," he said with disgust. "Rebels are tearing down the delicate agreement we have in place."

I remained silent; it wasn't my job to question him and would only anger him. I knew of the agreement. We were one of four cities that were allowed to survive after the Great War. Each was given a different way to rule over its citizens. The only rule is that each city must remain under the control of the chosen bloodline. Our lives were a game for an unforeseen player who, in exchange for our following the rules and remaining loyal, allowed us to survive.

"The bloodline rulers remain intact, but they disrespect the accord," he continued with a look of disgust. "So, daughter," he snarled. "Do you plan to join this movement?"

"I don't understand, my King," I said as smoothly as a lady should.

"Don't play dumb!" My father yelled, slamming his hand down on the throne. "It is your generation destroying everything! Is that your plan?! Kill me, take over, and fight against the one thing that has kept us all alive?!"

Keeping my voice free of emotion, I allowed his words to settle in. Yes, once I was a ruler, I wanted to make changes. But I had no intentions of assassinating him or going against the agreement. I had no idea what had led the others to do so, but it was not my intention.

Slowly, I lowered myself to my knees and bowed again. "You are my king," I said in a steady voice. "I pray for your long reign that only ends when you are called to the kingdom in the sky to join our ancestors. I respect and will uphold our traditions until my dying breath."

The king instantly relaxed and motioned for me to stand. I did with all the grace I had been taught over my twenty-two years of life.

"I had to be sure," he sighed. "As you are aware, we have those in our kingdom who say it is time for change. A rebellion is forming outside our walls, gathering numbers every day and putting everything we have at risk."

I stood still as a statue as he motioned, and a man stepped forward.

"You will be a target," the king said firmly. There was no concern in his voice. In truth, he felt nothing for me. I was just a necessary tool to keep things going. "If you are killed or swayed, everything will come to an end. I am assigning you a personal guard."

My eyes glided over to the man. He was dressed more like an assassin than a guard. His clothes were loose-fitting, and he wore no metal armor.

"He will be by your side always," the king ordered.

"Princess." The man stepped forward and bowed to me before straightening. He looked into my eyes, a small smirk playing on his lips.

A tingling instantly spread through my skin. I had never seen him in court before. Something was different about him, and it put all my nerves on edge. There would be no escaping him, not if he was ordered to always be by side. Too bad for him. He probably thought I was just a spoiled princess whom he could toy with. If nothing else, I could have a bit of fun toying with him.

Dear Reader,

Thank you for joining me on yet another adventure. I know the world is full of options regarding what you could spend your time reading and I am honored you chose my book. Please be sure to leave a review as these help me to reach more readers (and make me smile).

If you are ready for another adventure or want to keep up to date with new releases, please join me on my socials.

J.D. Crist

www.ingramcontent.com/pod-product-compliance
Lightning Source LLC
LaVergne TN
LVHW032007070526
838202LV00059B/6332